C0063 66741

KT-449-795

Dear Stranger,

If you're reading this letter, it's most likely you're reading my book. Hello. It's nice to meet you.

The idea for this book came from a lot of different places. A part of it arrived around my birthday one year, when I received an anonymous text telling me to check my letter box. I checked it straight away – I was between book ideas – and found a sandwich bag full of cut up Pablo Neruda poetry, with instructions: I was to use the lines of poetry to make a new poem and post it within twenty-four hours.

Other messages came over the following weeks. One sent me to the state library, where my sender had hidden messages in books that were shelved in the permanent collection. I had forty-eight hours to find them. I located all but one.

As it turned out, the sender of my secret messages was my best friend. (She's always been great at keeping secrets.) Apparently, I'd lost my love of words. She'd decided to help me find it.

I did find that love again. I found it in libraries and secondhand bookstores, where I went after her messages stopped. I thought about that one message I didn't find. Who found it? And what was their story? I thought about all the things left in books – lists, notes, dreams, thoughts. And I began a story about the things readers leave behind.

When my dad became sick, he mailed me copies of the books that he'd read so I could read them and we could talk. Those books arrived smelling of tobacco and old woollen jumpers. In some books he'd left the wrappers of sweets. They arrived covered with his thoughts, too, visible only to me. Those things were precious before he died, but even more so after.

I hope you enjoy *Words in Deep Blue*. Leave a letter for someone else in this book, or leave a note in the margin.

Or don't.

You'll be on the pages anyway.

CATH CROWLEY

Words in Deep Blue

—

CATH CROWLEY

Hodder
Children's
Books

HODDER CHILDREN'S BOOKS

First published in Great Britain in 2018 by Hodder and Stoughton

First published in the USA by Alfred A. Knopf Books for Young Readers in 2017

1 3 5 7 9 10 8 6 4 2

Text copyright © Cath Crowley 2017

The moral right of the author has been asserted.

*All characters and events in this publication, other than those clearly
in the public domain, are fictitious and any resemblance to
real persons, living or dead, is purely coincidental.*

All rights reserved.
No part of this publication may be reproduced, stored in
a retrieval system, or transmitted, in any form or by any means, without
the prior permission in writing of the publisher, nor be otherwise circulated
in any form of binding or cover other than that in which it is published
and without a similar condition including this condition being
imposed on the subsequent purchaser.

A CIP catalogue record for this book
is available from the British Library.

ISBN 978 1 444 90789 6

Printed and bound by CPI Group (UK) Ltd, Croydon, CR0 4YY

The paper and board used in this book
are made from wood from responsible sources.

MIX
Paper from
responsible sources
FSC® C104740

Hodder Children's Books
An imprint of
Hachette Children's Group
Part of Hodder and Stoughton
Carmelite House
50 Victoria Embankment
London EC4Y 0DZ

An Hachette UK Company
www.hachette.co.uk

www.hachettechildrens.co.uk

For Michael Crowley and
Michael Kitson, game changers

A book must be the ax for the frozen sea inside us. —KAFKA

The Pale King

by David Foster Wallace

Marking found on p. 585

Every love story is a ghost story.

Prufrock and Other Observations

by T. S. Eliot

Letter left between pp. 4 and 5
December 12, 2012

Dear Henry,

I'm leaving this letter on the same page as 'The Love Song of J. Alfred Prufrock' because you love the poem, and I love you. I know you're out with Amy, but fuck it – she doesn't love you, Henry. She loves herself, quite a bit, in fact. And I love you. I love that you read. I love that you love secondhand books. I love pretty much everything about you, and I've known you for ten years, so that's saying something. I leave tomorrow. Please call me when you get this, no matter how late.

Rachel

Rachel

I open my eyes at midnight to the sound of the ocean and my brother's breathing. It's been ten months since Cal drowned, but the dreams still escape.

I'm confident in the dreams, liquid with the sea. I'm breathing underwater, eyes open and unstung by salt. I see fish, a school of silver-bellied moons thrumming beneath me. Cal appears, ready to identify, but these aren't fish we know. 'Mackerel,' he says, his words escaping in bubbles that I can hear. But the fish aren't mackerel. Not bream, not any of the names we offer. They're pure silver. 'An unidentified species,' we say as we watch them fold and unfold around us. The water has the texture of sadness: salt and heat and memory.

Cal is in the room when I wake. He's milky-skinned in the darkness, dripping of ocean. Impossible, but so real I smell salt and apple gum. So real I see the scar on his right foot – a long-healed cut from glass on the beach. He's talking about the dream fish: pure silver, unidentified and gone.

The room is dark except for the moonlight. I feel through the air for the dream, but instead I touch the ears of Cal's Labrador, Woof. He follows me everywhere since the funeral, a long line of black I can't shake.

Usually, he sleeps on the end of my bed or in the doorway of my room, but for the last two nights he's slept in front of my packed suitcases. I can't take him with me. 'You're an ocean dog.' I run my finger along his nose. 'You'd go mad in the city.'

There's no sleeping after dreams of Cal, so I pull on clothes and climb out the window. The moon is three-quarters empty. The air is as hot as day. I mowed late yesterday, so I collect warm blades of grass on the soles of my feet as I move.

Woof and I get to the beach quickly. There's almost nothing between our house and the water. There's the road, a small stretch of scrub, and then dunes. The night is all tangle and smell. Salt and tree; smoke from a fire far up the beach. It's all memory, too. Summer swimming and night walks, hunts for fig shells and blennies and starfish.

Farther, toward the lighthouse, there's the spot where the beaked whale washed ashore: a giant at six meters, the right side of its face pressed against sand, its one visible eye open. There was a crowd of people around it later – scientists and locals studying and staring. But first there was Mum and Cal and me in the early cold. I was nine years old, and with its long beak it looked to me like it was half sea creature, half bird. I wanted to study the deep water it had come from, the things it might have seen. Cal and I spent the day looking through Mum's books and on the internet.

The beaked whale is considered one of the least understood creatures of the sea, I copied into my journal. *They live at depths so deep that the pressure could kill.*

I don't believe in ghosts or past lives or time travel or any of the strange things that Cal liked to read about. But every time I stand on the beach, I wish us back – to the day of the whale, to any day before Cal died. With what I know, I'd be ready. I'd save him.

It's late, but there'll be people from school out, so I walk farther up to a quiet spot. I dig myself into the dunes, burying my legs past my hips, and stare at the water. It's shot with moon, silver leaking all over the surface.

I've tried and tried to stop thinking about the day Cal drowned, but I can't. I hear his words. I hear his footsteps through the sand. I see him diving: a long, frail arc that disappears into sea.

I'm not sure how long I've been here when I see Mum walking over the dunes, her feet struggling to find traction. She sits on one side of me and lights a cigarette, cupping it from the night.

She started smoking again after Cal died. I found her and Dad hiding behind the church after the funeral. 'Don't say it, Rach,' she said, and I stood between them and held their free hands, wishing Cal had been there to see the strangeness of our parents smoking. Dad's a doctor; he's been working with Doctors Without Borders since the divorce ten years ago. Mum's a science teacher at the high school in Sea Ridge. They've called cigarettes 'death sticks' all our lives.

We watch the water without talking for a while. I don't know how Mum feels about the ocean now. She doesn't go in anymore, but we meet at the edge every night. She taught Cal and me how to swim, how to cup water, how to push it back and control its flow. She told us not to be afraid. 'Don't ever swim alone, though,' she said, and apart from that one time, we didn't.

'So, you're packed?' Mum asks, and I nod.

Tomorrow I leave Sea Ridge for Gracetown, a suburb of Melbourne, the city where my aunt Rose lives. I've failed Year 12, and since I don't plan to try again next year, Rose has gotten me a job in the café at St. Albert's Hospital, where she's a doctor.

Cal and I grew up in Gracetown. We moved to Sea Ridge three years ago, when I was fifteen. Gran needed help, and we didn't want her to sell the house or go into a home. We'd stayed with her every holiday, summer and winter, since we were born, so Sea Ridge was like our second home.

'Year 12 isn't everything,' Mum says.

Maybe it's not, but before Cal died, I had my life planned. I got As, I was happy. I sat on this exact spot last year and told Cal I wanted to be an ichthyologist, studying fish like the Chimaera, which evolved 400 million years ago. We both tried to imagine a world that went that far back.

'I feel like the universe cheated Cal and cheated us along with him,' I say now.

Before Cal died, Mum would have explained calmly and logically that the universe was all existing matter and space – 10 billion light-years in diameter, consisting of galaxies and the solar system, stars and the planets. All of which simply do not have the capacity to cheat a person of anything.

Tonight she lights another cigarette. 'It did,' she says, and blows smoke at the stars.

Henry

I'm lying next to Amy in the self-help section of Howling Books. We're alone. It's ten on Thursday night and I'll be honest: I'm currently mismanaging a hard-on. The mismanagement isn't entirely my fault. My body's working on muscle memory.

Usually, this is the time and place that Amy and I kiss. This is the time our hearts breathe hard and she lies next to me, warm-skinned and funny, making jokes about the state of my hair. It's the time we talk about the future, which was, if you'd asked me fifteen minutes ago, completely bought and paid for.

'I want to break up,' she says, and at first I think she's joking. Less than twelve hours ago, we were kissing in this exact spot. We were doing quite a few other very nice things too, I think, as she elbows me.

'Henry?' she says. 'Say something.'

'Say what?' I ask.

'I don't know. Whatever you're thinking.'

'I'm thinking this is entirely unexpected and a little bit shit.' I struggle into an upright position. 'We bought plane tickets. Nonrefundable, nonexchangeable plane tickets for the twelfth of March.'

'I know, Henry,' she says.

'We leave in *ten* weeks.'

'Calm down,' she says, as though I'm the one who's sounding unreasonable. Maybe I am sounding unreasonable, but that's because I spent the last dollar of my savings buying a six-stop-around-the-world ticket. Singapore, Berlin, Rome, London, Helsinki, New York. 'We bought travel insurance and got our passports. We bought travel guides and those little blow pillows for the plane.'

She bites the right side of her lip, and I try very hard, unsuccessfully, not to think about kissing her. 'You said you loved me.'

'I do love you,' Amy says, and then she starts italicizing love into all its depressing definitions. 'I just don't think I'm *in* love with you. I tried, though. I tried *really* hard.'

These must be the most depressing words in the history of love. *I tried really hard to love you.* I'm not certain of a lot of things, but I'm certain of this – when I'm old and I have dementia, when my brain has aged to smoke, these are words I will remember.

I should ask her to leave. I should say, 'You know what? I don't want to see the homelands of William Shakespeare and Mary Shelley and Friedrich Nietzsche and Jane Austen and Emily Dickinson and Karen Russell with a girl who's trying very hard to love me.' I should say, 'If you don't love me, then I don't love you.'

But fuck it I do love her and I would like to see those homelands with her and I'm an optimist without a whole lot of dignity, so what I say is 'If you change your mind, you know where

I live.' In my defense she's crying and we've been friends since Year 9 and in my book that counts for a lot.

There's no other way for her to leave but to climb over me, because the self-help section is in a small room at the back of the shop that most people think is a closet, but it's just big enough for two people to lie side by side with no space to spare.

We do this weird fumbling dance as she gets up, a soft untangling wrestle. We kiss before she goes. It's a long kiss, a good kiss, and while it's happening I let myself hope that maybe, just maybe, it's so great that it's changed her mind.

But after it's done, she stands and straightens her skirt and gives me a small, sad wave. And then she leaves me here, lying on the floor of the self-help section – a dead man. One with a nonrefundable, nonexchangeable ticket to the world.

Eventually I crawl out of the self-help section and make my way to the fiction couch: the long blue velvet daybed that sits in front of the classics shelves. I rarely sleep upstairs anymore. I like the rustle and dust of the bookshop at night.

I lie here thinking about Amy. I retrace last week, running back through the hours, trying to work out what changed between us. But I'm the same person I was seven days ago. I'm the same person I was the week before and the week before that. I'm the same person I was all the way back to the morning we met.

Amy came from a private school across the river and moved to our side of town when her dad's accounting firm downsized and he had to shift jobs. They lived in one of the new apartments that had gone up on Green Street, not far from the school. From Amy's new bedroom, she could hear traffic and the flush of next-door's toilet. From her old bedroom, she could hear birds. These things I learned before we dated, in snippets of conversations that happened on the way home from parties, in English, in detention, in the library, when she stopped by the bookshop on Sunday afternoons.

The first day I met her I knew surface things – she had long red hair, green eyes and fair skin. She smelled flowery. She wore long socks. She sat at an empty table and waited for people to sit next to her. They did.

I sat in front and listened to the conversation between her and Aaliyah. 'Who's that?' I heard Amy ask. 'Henry,' Aaliyah told her. 'Funny. Smart. Cute.'

I waved above my head at them, without turning around.

'An eavesdropper,' Amy added, gently kicking the back of my chair.

We didn't officially get together till the middle of Year 12, but the first time we kissed was in Year 9. It happened after our English class had been studying Ray Bradbury's short stories. After we read 'The Last Night of the World', the idea caught on that we should all spend a night pretending it was *our* last and do the things we'd do if an apocalypse was heading our way.

Our English teacher heard what we were planning, and the principal told us we couldn't do it. It sounded dangerous. Our plans went underground. Flyers appeared in lockers that the date was set for the twelfth of December, the last day of school before summer vacation. There'd be a party that night at Justin Kent's house. MAKE PLANS, the flyers told us. THE END IS NEAR.

I stayed up late on the night before the end, trying to write the perfect letter to Amy, a letter that'd convince her to spend her last night in the world with me. I walked into school with it in my top pocket, knowing I probably wouldn't give it to her but hoping that I would. My plan was to spend the last night with friends unless some miracle happened and Amy became a possibility.

No one listened in class that day. There were small signs all over the place that things were coming to an end. In our homeroom, someone had turned all the notices on the board upside down. Someone had carved THE END into the back of the boys' toilet door. I opened my locker at lunch to find a piece of paper with ONE DAY TO GO written on it, and I realized that no one had bothered working out the finer details of when the world would actually end: Midnight? Sunrise?

I was thinking about that when I turned and saw Amy standing next to me. The note was in my pocket, but I couldn't give it to her. Instead, I held up the paper – ONE DAY TO GO – and asked her what she was planning to do with her last night. She stared at me for a while and eventually said, 'I thought you might ask me to spend it with you.' There were several people in the corridor listening, and all of us, me included, couldn't believe my luck.

To give myself maximum living time, I decided that the world should end when the sun came up – five fifty in the morning, according to the Weather Channel.

We met at the bookshop at five fifty in the afternoon to make it an even twelve hours, and from there we walked to Shanghai Dumplings for dinner. Around nine we went to Justin's party, and when it got too loud, we walked to the Benito Building and took the elevator to the top – the highest place in Gracetown.

We sat on my jacket and watched the lights, and she told me about her flat, the smallness of her room, the birds that she'd swapped for the toilet. It'd be years before Amy would tell me about the strangeness she felt when she heard her dad crying about his lost job. Then she only hinted at her family's worries. I offered her the bookshop if she ever needed space. Occasionally there'd be bird sounds if she sat in the reading garden. The sounds of turning pages are surprisingly comforting, I told her.

She kissed me then, and even though we didn't date till years later, something started in that moment. Every now and then, when she was alone at the end of a party, we'd kiss again. Girls knew, even if Amy was with some other guy at the time, that I belonged to her.

In Year 12, Amy came to the bookshop one night. We were closed. I was studying behind the counter. She'd been going out with a guy called Ewan, who went to school in her old neighborhood. I liked those kinds of guys because I rarely had to see them. Ewan had broken up with her, and Amy needed someone she could rely on to take her to the formal. So there she was at the door of the bookshop, tapping on the glass, and calling my name.

Rachel

Mum goes back to the house, but I stay on the beach with Woof. I take out the letter I've been carrying around since I decided to go back to the city – the last letter that Henry wrote to me. After I moved to Sea Ridge, Henry wrote every week for about three months until he got the message that we weren't friends anymore.

'There's no point writing back unless he tells me the truth,' I'd say to Cal every time I got a letter, and every time Cal would stare at me, eyes serious behind his glasses, and say something like, 'It's Henry. Henry, your best friend, Henry who helped us build the tree house that time, Henry who helped us both in English, *Henry.*'

'You left out shithead,' I'd remind him. 'Henry who is a shithead.'

It wasn't really a problem that I was Henry's best friend and in love with him at the same time until the beginning of Year 9. He got small crushes on other girls but he didn't act on them and they didn't last and I was the one he sat with and called late at night.

But then Amy arrived. She had red hair and this impossible skin with not a single freckle. I'm covered in a soft dust from years of summers at the beach. Amy was smart, too. We competed for the math prize that year, and she won. I won the science prize. She won Henry.

She told me she would, on the day before summer vacation. We'd been studying the writer Ray Bradbury in English. One of his short stories was about a couple on their last night before the world ends, and the idea had spread around that we should all imagine it was *our* last night. Really it was an excuse for hookups; a free pass to tell whomever it was that you loved, that you loved them. I wasn't planning on telling Henry, but since it was also my last night in the city, he said we should spend it together.

'You like him,' Amy said, looking at me in the bathroom mirror that morning.

Henry and I had met way back in the primary school car pool. I can't remember that first conversation, but I remember other ones: books, the planets, time travel, kissing, sex, the circumference of the moon. It felt as though I knew everything there was to know about Henry. *Like* just didn't seem to cover it.

'He's my best friend,' I told her.

'I'm asking him,' she said, and I knew what she meant.

'He's spending it with me,' I told her.

Henry told me that afternoon that Amy wanted him to spend the last night of the world with her. We were lying on the grass at lunch, watching insects skate on lines of sun. 'I said yes, but if it really bothers you, I can go back and say no.' Then he got on his knees and begged for me to let him spend the last night of the world with her.

I closed my eyes and told him it was fine.

'What else could I say?' I asked Lola that night. 'I'm in love with you and I have been forever and if there are two people who should *definitely* spend the last night of the world together, it's us. Henry and Rachel.'

'Why not?' she asked, sitting cross-legged on my bed, eating chocolate. 'I mean really, why the fuck not? Why not just say you, *you*, my friend, are the person I want to kiss?'

Lola was a good friend but she was *Lola Hero*, the girl who wrote songs and played bass, the girl who people listed when they listed people they'd like to be. If she liked a girl, she asked her out the same day. The kind of love she wrote about wasn't the kind of love people like me experienced.

Why not? 'Because I am not a huge fan of failure and humiliation.'

But by eleven that night, after a tub of ice cream, a bag of marshmallows, and three blocks of chocolate, this kind of madness hit and I decided to break into Howling Books and leave a love letter for Henry in the Letter Library.

My world seemed too small that night. The air on the way pressed on my skin and the inside of me pressed out. I'd never even hinted to Henry that I liked him, but with the clock ticking down to the end of the world, it became the thing I had to do before that last second – and the Letter Library was the perfect way to do it.

It's a section of books that aren't for sale. Customers can read the books, but they can't take them home. The idea is that they can circle words or phrases on the pages of their favorite books. They can write notes in the margins. They can leave letters for other people who've read the same books.

Henry loves the Letter Library. So does his whole family. I didn't quite see the point of writing to a stranger in a book. There's a much better chance of getting a reply from a stranger if you write to them online. Henry always said that if I didn't understand the Library, then he couldn't explain it. The Letter Library was something I had to get instinctively.

There wasn't an alarm on the bookstore, and the lock on the toilet window that faced on to Charmers Street was broken. Lola and I climbed through and listened before we left the bathroom to make sure no one was in the store.

I put the letter in T. S. Eliot's *Prufrock and Other Observations*, on the page of Henry's favorite poem: 'The Love Song of J. Alfred Prufrock.' I remember the circle of the flashlight as I searched for it on the shelves. My hands shook as I wrote the letter. It was mostly *I love you* – a little *go fuck yourself.* The perfect love letter, according to Lola.

I could have left everything to chance, but I decided that if I was doing this, I was really doing it. I climbed silently upstairs to Henry's room. His latest book was on his bed. I left a note in it:

Look in the Prufrock tonight. —Rachel

Lola and I went silently back out the bathroom window, holding our breath the whole way, laughing as we hit the street. We shared a cab home, and by the time I arrived at my place, I was already obsessively checking my phone. I fell asleep waiting.

Lola woke me around three, asking if Henry had called. He hadn't. He hadn't come around by the time we left at nine. At ten, when we were on the road, he sent me a text: Sorry, I overslept!! Will call soon.

Henry doesn't use exclamation marks. He doesn't like the look of them unless they fill a whole page, in which case they look like rain. If he has to use them, he never uses two. We had a whole conversation about it once that involved him listing the fourteen punctuation marks in order of his favorites. 'Ellipses,' according to Henry, are 'fucking excellent.' The exclamation mark is just a weird guy who talks too loudly.

Amy loves exclamation points. She wrote the text, I was sure of it. I imagined her reading my letter over Henry's shoulder and telling him how he should reply. 'Ignore it. She's leaving anyway.'

I wasn't angry with him for not being in love with me. A person can't help that. I was angry because he let Amy tell him what to do. He put her before me. Henry never replied to my letter. He never mentioned it in the long letters he wrote, which I ignored because they were full of Amy.

Henry doesn't know about Cal. If he did, I'm sure nothing would have kept him from the funeral. But I haven't told him and neither has Mum. Rose can't say the words without crying and she never cries in public. Cal wasn't on Facebook. He had an account, but he wasn't interested.

Tim Hooper, his best friend from Gracetown, moved to Western Australia a couple of months before Cal died, so I wrote him a letter with the news. I didn't need to tell him not to post it on social media. I didn't have to say that I couldn't stand the idea that Cal's death would be gossip for people to comment on. Tim just knew.

. . .

Part of me wants to walk into Howling Books as soon as I arrive. I could walk up to Henry and tell him about Cal and he'd put down the book he was reading and he'd hug me.

But I open his letter and read the first two lines and all the anger comes back.

> *Dear Rachel,*
> *Since you never write, I can only assume you've forgotten me. Again, I refer you to the blood oath we took in Grade 3.*

I fold up the letter, and with the help of Woof, I dig a hole and bury it in the sand.

Henry

I wake Friday morning to see my sister, George, standing next to the fiction couch, where I fell asleep last night, and where I plan to keep sleeping all week.

Not surprisingly, I haven't taken the breakup well, and I have no plans to take it well in the future. My plan is to stay on the couch, getting up for toilet breaks and the occasional toasted sandwich until Amy comes back to me. She always comes back to me. It's just a matter of time.

I collected all the books I thought I'd need before I took to the couch, so they're all piled up around me – there's some Patrick Ness, an Ernest Cline, some Gaiman, Flannery O'Connor, John Green, Nick Hornby, some Kelly Link, and, if all else fails, Douglas Adams.

'Get. Up,' George says, gently shoving me with her knee, which is her version of a hug. I love my sister, but, along with the rest of the world, I don't really understand her and it'd be true to say I fear her, just slightly.

She's seventeen, starting Year 12 this year. She likes learning, but she hates her school. She got a scholarship to a private one on the other side of the river in Year 7, and Mum makes her stay there even though she'd rather go to Gracetown High.

She wears a huge amount of black, and T-shirts with things like READ, MOTHERFUCKERS on the front. Sometimes I think she likes post-apocalyptic fiction so much because she's genuinely happy at the thought that the world might end.

'Is the plan to get up sometime soon?' she asks, and I tell her no, that is not the plan. I explain the plan to her, which is basically to wait, horizontally, for life to improve.

She's holding a brown paper bag soft with grease, though, and I'm fairly certain it has a sugar-and-cinnamon donut inside, so I sit up. 'At this point I don't have anything to get up for,' I say, reaching into the bag.

'No one has anything to get up for. Life's pointless and everyone just gets up anyway. That's how the human race works,' she says, and hands me a coffee.

'I don't like how the human race works.'

'No one likes how the human race works,' she says.

I finish eating and lie back on the bed, staring at the ceiling. 'I have a nonrefundable round-the-world ticket.'

'So go see the world,' George says as Dad walks past.

'Get up, Henry,' he says. 'You're fermenting. Tell him he's fermenting, George.'

'You're fermenting,' George says, and pushes me over so she can sit next to me. She lifts my legs and puts them over her legs.

'I don't understand,' Dad says. 'You were such happy children.'

'I was never a happy child,' George says.

'True, but Henry was.'

'I'm not anymore. It's actually hard to imagine how my life could be any shittier at this point,' I say, and George holds up the copy of the book she's reading. *The Road.*

'OK. Sure. It could get shittier if there was some kind of world-ending event and people started eating each other. But that's a whole different shit scale. On your average human-emotion scale, my life is registering as the shittiest of the shit.'

'There'll be other girls, Henry,' Dad says.

'Why does everyone keep saying that? I don't want other girls. I want this girl. I want this one. This girl. Not another one. This one.'

'Amy doesn't love you.' George says it gently – like she's sympathetically sticking a piece of glass straight through my left eye.

Amy does love me. She did love me. She wanted to spend an indefinite amount of time with me, and that's basically the same as forever. 'If a person wants to spend forever with you, that's love.'

'But she didn't want to spend forever with you,' George says.

'*Now. Now* she doesn't want to spend forever with me, but then she did, and forever doesn't just disappear overnight.' If it does, then there should be some sort of scientific law against it.

'He's flipping out,' George says.

'Take a shower, son,' Dad says.

'Give me one good reason.'

'You're working today,' he says, and I take my heartbroken self off to the bathroom.

According to George, it's a truth universally acknowledged that our family is shit at love. Even our cat, Ray Bradbury, she points out, doesn't seem to get it on with the other cats in the neighborhood.

Mum and Dad have tried six times to get back together, but, finally, last year they signed the divorce papers and Mum moved out of the bookshop into a small flat in Renwood, a couple of suburbs away. When George isn't at school, she spends all her time sitting in the window of the shop writing in her journal. Dad's been on the down side since Mum left, with no sign of stopping his post-divorce habit of eating whole blocks of peppermint chocolate every night while he rereads Dickens.

I don't agree with George. It's not that I think we're great at love, but I think the whole world is fairly shit at it, so, statistically speaking, we're average, and I can live with that.

Amy did love me. Sure, she leaves me every now and then, but she always comes back. You don't keep coming back to someone you don't love.

I stand in the shower and try to work out what I did wrong. There must have been a moment when I messed it up, and if I could find my way back to it, maybe that moment could be fixed.

Why? I text Amy after I've dried off. There must be a reason. Can you at least tell me that?

I press Send and head downstairs to the shop.

. . .

'He looks better,' Dad says when I rejoin them.

George looks up, grimaces, and decides it's best not to answer.

'What's that wonderful Dickens line from *Great Expectations*?' Dad asks. *'The broken heart. You think you will die, but you just keep living, day after day after terrible day.'*

'That's hugely comforting, Dad,' George says.

'The terrible days get better,' he tells us, but he doesn't sound all that convincing.

'I'm going book hunting,' he says, which is unusual for a Friday. I ask if he wants some company, but he waves me off and tells me to look after the shop. 'I'll see you tonight – eight o'clock at Shanghai Dumplings.'

Since I finished Year 12 last November, I've worked in the bookshop every day. We sell secondhand books, which is the right kind of book to sell for this side of town. Dad and I do the book hunting. It's getting harder. Not harder to find books – books are everywhere and I've got my particular spots to look, spots Dad showed me – but harder to find the bargains. Everyone knows the worth of things these days, so you don't just find a first edition of *Casino Royale* sitting on someone's shelf that they don't know they've got. If you want to buy it, then you buy it for what it's worth.

I keep reading articles about the end of secondhand bookstores. Independent bookstores selling new books are hanging in there. Digital is obviously poised to thrive. But secondhand stores will be relics soon, apparently.

I've been thinking about this lately because, since the divorce, Mum's been talking about selling Howling Books. She and Dad bought the place twenty years ago, when it was a florist shop. It was priced cheaply for a quick sale. The owner had just walked out for some reason. When Mum and Dad came to inspect it, there were buckets still on the floor and the place smelled of flowers and moldy water. The bills were gone from the till, but there were still coins in the drawers.

Mum and Dad kept the wooden counter running along the right as you walk in, as well as the old green register and red lamp that the florist had left behind, but they changed almost everything else in the long, narrow space. They put in windows along the front of the store, and Dad and his brother, Jim, polished the floorboards. They built shelves that run floor to ceiling the whole length of the shop, and huge wooden ladders that lean against the shelves so people can reach the books at the top. They built the glassed-in shelves where we keep the first editions, and the waist-high shelves in the center of the store at the back. They built the shelves where we keep the Letter Library.

In the middle of the shop, in front of the counter, there's the specials table, and behind that is the fiction couch. At the back on the left are the stairs to our flat, on the right is the self-help cupboard, and then through the back glass doors is a reading garden. Jim covered it, so people can sit out there no matter what the weather, but he left the ivy and jasmine growing up the bluestone walls. In the garden there are tables with Scrabble boards and couches and chairs.

There's a stone wall on the right, and in that stone wall there's a locked door that leads through to Frank's Bakery. I've suggested to Frank that he should open it so people could buy coffee from him and then bring it into our garden, but Frank isn't interested. In the whole time I've known him, which is since I was born, he's never changed a thing in his shop. It's still got the same black-and-white tiles, the same diner-style counter with black leather stools along it. He makes the same pastries, he won't make soy lattes, and he plays Frank Sinatra all day.

He gives me my second coffee for the morning and tells me I look terrible. 'So I hear,' I say, putting in some sugar and stirring. 'Amy dumped me. I'm brokenhearted.'

'You don't know what brokenhearted is,' Frank says, and gives me a free blueberry Danish, burnt on the underside, just the way I like it.

I take my coffee and Danish back to the shop and start sorting through the books that need to be priced.

I check every single one of them, because what I like about secondhand books is that you find all kinds of things inside – coffee rings, circled words, notes in the margin. George and I have found a lot of stuff in books over the years – letters, shopping lists, bus tickets, dreams. I've found tiny spiders, flattened cigarettes, and stale tobacco in the creases. I found a condom once (wrapped and unused but ten years out of date – a story in itself). I once found a copy of *The Encyclopedia of World Flora 1958*. Someone had used leaves to mark the pages of their favorite plants. The leaves had dried to bones by the time I opened the book. All that was left were the skeletons.

Secondhand books are full of mysteries, which is why I like them.

Frederick walks in while I'm thinking that. He's a bit of a mystery himself. He's been a regular here since the day we opened. According to Mum and Dad, Frederick was our first official customer. He was fifty then, but he's seventy now, or thereabouts.

He's an elegant man who loves gray suits, deep-blue ties, and Derek Walcott.

I'm fond of Derek Walcott too. I could eat his poem 'Love After Love'. Just peel the words off the page and stuff them in my mouth.

For as long as I've been book hunting, as long as the shop's been open, Frederick has been looking for a particular edition of Walcott poems. He could order a new copy, but he's looking for a secondhand one. He's not looking for a first edition. He's looking for a particular book that he owned once, and something like that, he's likely never to find.

I don't think he should stop looking, though. Who am I to say he won't find it? The odds are stacked against him, but impossible things happen. Maybe I'll find it myself. Maybe it won't be too far from home. Secondhand books have a way of traveling, sure. But what travels forward can come back.

Frederick won't tell me what's in the Walcott. He's a private man, a polite man, with the saddest eyeballs I've ever seen.

I hand him the three copies I've found over the last month, and he dismisses the first two, but hesitates over the third. From the way he holds it in his hands, I wonder if maybe I've found the one. He opens the cover, turns the pages, and then tries not to look disappointed.

He takes out his wallet, and I tell him he doesn't have to keep buying the books if I haven't found the right one. 'They sell, and I'll go on looking for you anyway.'

He insists, though, and I imagine someone walking into Frederick's house after he's died and finding hundreds of versions of the same Walcott book, and wondering why they're there.

Frederick isn't the only regular. There's Al, who reads a lot of science fiction and looks like someone who does. He's been working for years on a novel about a guy who's jacked into a virtual utopia. We're all searching for a way to tell him that it's already been written. There's James, who comes in to buy books on the Romans. There's Aaron, who arrives drunk at least once every couple of months, banging on the door late at night, because he needs to use the bathroom; Inez, who just seems to like the smell of old books; and Jett, who comes in to steal the hardcover books so he can sell them to any other secondhand place that'll take them.

There's Frieda, who's been playing Scrabble here with Frederick for ten years. She's about Frederick's age and wears severe stylish dresses, and you just know she used to be one of those English teachers who scared the crap out of her students. She's in the monthly book club, which Howling Books hosts but doesn't run.

The same people come every time. I set up the chairs, open the door, put out a whole lot of wine and cheese, and then stand back. I hardly ever join in the discussion, but if it interests me, which it pretty much always does, I read the book afterward. Last month they read Kirsty Eagar's *Summer Skin*. George read it after the book club because they'd talked about the sex scenes, and maybe I read it a little for that reason too. But mostly I read it because of the way Frieda talked about the main character, Jess Gordon. She reminded me, a little, of a best friend I had once called Rachel Sweetie. I liked the book – George did too – so we put a copy in the Letter Library.

The Library is the thing that Howling Books is known for, at least locally. We get a write-up every now and then, on sites like Broadsheet, as something special to do in the city.

It's up in the back, near the stairs to our flat. It's separate from the rest of the shelves. In it we keep copies of books that people particularly love – fiction, nonfiction, romance and sci-fi, poetry and atlases, and cookbooks. Customers are allowed to write in the books in the Letter Library. They can circle words that they love, highlight lines. They can leave notes in the margins, thoughts about the meaning of things. We've had to get multiple copies of books by people like Tom Stoppard and John Green because *Rosencrantz and Guildenstern Are Dead* and *The Fault in Our Stars* are crammed with notes from readers.

It's called the Letter Library because a lot of people write more than a note in the margin – they write whole letters and put them between the pages of books. Letters to the poets, to their thief ex-boyfriend or ex-girlfriend who stole their copy of *High Fidelity*. Mostly people write to strangers who love the same books as them – and some stranger, somewhere, writes back.

Pride and Prejudice and Zombies

by Jane Austen and Seth Grahame-Smith

Letters left between pp. 44 and 45
November 23–December 7, 2012

Written on title page: *This book belongs to George Jones. So don't sell it in the bookstore, Henry.*

Dear George,

You're probably surprised to find this letter in your book. Maybe you're wondering how it got here. I'll leave that a mystery.

I haven't actually left it, yet – I'm still in my room writing it – and I'm sure getting it into the pages wasn't easy. I'm thinking I'll put it in when you've excused yourself from class to go to the bathroom and left the book on your desk. But I know you like to find things in secondhand books, so I'll give it my best shot. And here it is, so I must have been successful.

I don't plan on telling you who I am, at least not right away. I'm a guy, your age, in at least one of your classes.

If you'd like to write back, you can put this book into the Letter Library at your bookstore and leave a letter between pages 44 and 45.

I'm not a stalker. I like books. (I like you.)

> *Pytheas (obviously not my real name)*

Pytheas - or Stacy, or whichever friend of hers wrote this,

Stay away from me. If I catch you in my shop, I'll call the police.

> George

Dear George,

Thank you for writing back, even if only to tell me that you plan to call the police on me.

I don't want to make you angry, but I'm not one of Stacy's friends. I don't really like Stacy and she definitely doesn't like me. This isn't a joke. You're funny and smart and I'd really like to write to you.

> *Pytheas (Would any of Stacy's friends call themselves Pytheas?)*

Pytheas,

> *So you're not a friend of Stacy's? Prove it.*
>
>   *George*

Dear George,

That's a hard one. How can I prove to you I'm not playing a joke? If we were a mathematical equation, then it would be easy. But you might just have to take a chance.

I'll tell you some things about me. Maybe that would help? I like science. I like math. I like solving problems. I believe in ghosts. I'm particularly interested in time travel and space and the ocean.

I haven't decided what I want to do when I leave school, but I think I'll either study the ocean or space. Before that, I think I'll travel. The first place I want to go is the Atacama Desert. It's 1,000 kilometers, running from Peru's southern border into Chile. It faces on to the South Pacific Ocean and it's known as the driest place on earth. There are parts where it has never rained. Things don't rot without moisture. So if something died in there, it would be preserved forever. You can see on page 50 of the atlas in the Letter Library. (I've also marked some other places I want to see in South America.)

Will you tell me some things about you?

>   *Pytheas*

Pytheas,

   Why are you writing to me? According to everyone at school, I'm a freak.

George

Dear George,

   I quite like freaks.

Pytheas

Rachel

I drive out of Sea Ridge early on Friday afternoon in Gran's car. It's old – a 1990s dark blue Volvo – but at least it's mine. It was Gran's idea for me to move in with Rose, and as a way of tempting me to go, she gave me transport.

In one of our sessions Gus, my grief counselor, asked me to imagine how I'd feel leaving the ocean. 'Light,' I'd told him. 'Relieved.' I wouldn't have to run into my ex-boyfriend, Joel, or the teachers I'd disappointed, or the friends I'd drifted away from. I wouldn't have to see people from the beach lifeguard club where I'd worked before Cal died, or the kids I'd taught to swim at the local pool.

I don't feel light or relieved today, though. For one thing, I haven't driven much since I got my license and Gran's car isn't automatic and it doesn't seem to go much faster than forty miles per hour.

And then there's the box of Cal's stuff that Gran put in the trunk before I left. I hate that Cal's life ended as a set of boxes with things written on the side like SPORTING GOODS, HOBBIES, COMPUTER EQUIPMENT and ENTERTAINMENT. Gran packed them at around the six-month mark.

The box in the car is full of items Gran can't categorize, so she wants me to go through it. There's a question mark on the side and the word MISCELLANEOUS written under that. I have this feeling I'll be driving around with it in the trunk for as long as I have this car.

I almost pull over at the thought, and hurl it from the cliffs. One good throw and it'd be gone for good. Everything's working against me, though – the color of sky, the light.

It's the exact time of day that Mum, Cal and I arrived here three years ago. We looked for the ocean as we approached, the way we always did, spotting it first in small triangles and then in deep scoops.

Cal had one of his atlases open on his lap, an old one, drawn in the nineteenth century. He'd found it at a secondhand store that day. I turned to the backseat and saw him smoothing his hands across the pages of the Southern Ocean, paler at the edges, dark blue in the deep.

We pooled facts about it as we drove. Fourth-largest ocean. Covers 17,968 kilometers. Has an area of 20,327,000 square kilometers and an average depth of between 4,000 and 5,000 meters. I remember the three of us went quiet for a moment, excited by the scale.

I take the turn inland and push the car as fast as it will go. The shrubs and the water move backward in a blur, and I imagine that time is rewinding. Back to when the world was some other place. I look through the windshield and wait for the concrete and the absence of sea.

· · ·

It's getting dark by the time I arrive and I miss the first turnoff to Gracetown on the freeway, so I have to get off at the next exit. This means I have to drive back through Charlotte Hill along High Street, past Howling Books, which sits next door to Frank's Bakery.

I haven't been back to the city since we moved. I crawl along with the traffic and the strangest feeling – like I'm driving through a dream of my past. Small things have changed: Beat Clothing is now Gracetown Organics. The DVD store is now a café. Other than that, it's the same.

When I pull up level with Howling Books, Henry's sitting behind the counter on a stool: heels hooked on the bottom steel rung, elbows on knees, book in hands, completely focused. The only sign that three years have passed is that I don't want to kiss him. There's a mild urge to kick him, but that's about it.

Before the traffic moves, Henry comes outside to take in the books from the street. The breeze shifts his hair around. It's got that same blue-black shine. I watch him and test myself, but no matter how I stare, there's no haze in my chest, no flicker in the skies.

I think back to those first few months in Sea Ridge, when every time I thought about him I burned with anger and embarrassment. When the only thing that took the blush off my skin was the sea.

Rose lives a block back from High Street, which is crammed with shops selling coffee and clothes and records. The north of the city always felt like the secondhand side of town to Cal and me, and we liked it. Over the river, in the south, there are wide streets and new clothes, but I prefer it here, with the cinema showing old and new films, the paintings on the side of buildings, the crooked power lines that crisscross the sky.

Rose's last flat, over the road from the hospital, only had one bedroom. When Cal and I stayed there, she put a mattress on the living-room floor for us. Her new place is an orange-brick warehouse with CAR REPAIRS written in faded letters across the outside. There's a wooden door on the left and double wooden doors on the right, which must be where they drove the cars in.

Rose is my favorite aunt – she was Cal's too – but she has always been the most elusive. She appears and disappears. When she appeared in Sea Ridge, she was always mowing the lawn or cleaning out the garage or smoking in the dunes. When she disappeared, it was always to somewhere exotic – traveling through Africa, working in London, volunteering in Chile.

Once I asked her why she didn't have kids.

'I never wanted them,' she said. 'I'm too busy. Plus, I swear too fucking much.'

But I know she didn't mind Cal and me being around. I'm told that after I was born, I cried all the time, so Rose would stop by after her shift at the hospital and hold me so Mum and Dad could get some sleep. Mum would get up in the night and hear Rose reciting the periodic table to me. 'It's the only story I know,' she'd said.

Before I get out of the car, I send Mum and Gran a quick text to let them know I've arrived, and then I take my suitcases out of the trunk. I leave Cal's box where it is, lock it inside.

'I heard she gave you the car,' Rose says when she opens the door. 'How'd it feel to drive here?'

'Pretty good.'

'You were scared the whole way, right?'

'Half the way,' I tell her, looking around.

'It's messy,' she says. 'I'm renovating.'

'There are no walls,' I say, and she taps on the outside one.

'There are no indoor walls.'

It's one huge room with polished concrete floors and walls of windows. There's a kitchen in the corner and two spaces set up as bedrooms.

I can see straight into Rose's life now. Her bed is unmade, a blue mess with a chest of drawers on one side and a shelf full of her medical books on the other. Her clothes, mostly jeans and T-shirts, are lying on the floor or half out of drawers. There's a clothes rack with some little black dresses, some long boots underneath it.

My corner of the warehouse is near the front windows. There's a bed with a pile of sheets on it, a chest of drawers, and an empty clothes rack.

'Obviously the long-term plan is to have walls, but until then we'll just have to respect each other's space. The bathroom has walls.' She points to a metal door near the kitchen. 'You don't like it?' she asks, watching me as I take the place in.

'I do. It's just not what I expected.'

But what I'm really thinking is, there's nowhere to hide.

I don't have much to unpack, and there's no food in the house, so Rose and I leave for the supermarket. I'm wondering on the way what I've gotten myself into. There's a slight buckling in my stomach every time I think about the openness of the warehouse.

I've grown used to being alone and doing my own thing – walking to the beach at night, skipping school to sleep, crying in my room where no one sees.

'I'm talking to you,' Rose says.

'And?'

'And you're not listening.' She points through the windshield. 'We're here. You get the shopping cart. I'll meet you inside.'

Rose isn't much of a cook, so we buy things that I can make or things we can heat up, and it feels good to be shopping in the city and not in Sea Ridge, where everyone knows everyone and everyone still gives us looks. This supermarket's new. Cal and I never stood in this chocolate aisle deliberating between peanut M&Ms and plain. Rose doesn't deliberate at all, as it turns out. She puts both bags in the cart.

'Your gran thinks you're not eating enough,' she says, and we keep moving. 'She also says you've turned into a zombie who hides in her room, sleeps all day, and spends her nights at the beach with her mother, who has also turned into a zombie.'

Rose throws cans of tuna in the cart while I'm checking myself out in the cake tins to see if I do actually look like the undead. The news isn't entirely good.

'She has no idea what a zombie actually is,' Rose says. 'I wouldn't worry.'

'Cal introduced her to zombies. *Shaun of the Dead* is her top movie of all time. Right up there with *Casablanca*.'

'We didn't even get to watch TV when I was growing up,' she says. 'Now she's watching Simon Pegg movies and telling me my niece needs to have sex.'

'What did you tell her?'

'That zombies don't have sex.'

Gran and Rose don't get along. They've fought for the sake of fighting all the way back to when Rose was three, so the family history goes. According to Gran, Rose swears too much, works too much, and doesn't come home nearly enough.

'If she sent you to me, you're in trouble,' Rose says.

'I tried to pass Year 12,' I say, in an effort to defend myself.

'If you'd been trying, you'd have passed. You could pass Year 12 with your eyes closed.'

I think of myself lying behind the school when I should have been in class – the sun on my face and the warm grass at my back. 'My eyes were closed most of the time.'

'Life starts again,' Rose says, as if that's something she can order.

We're carrying groceries back to the car when I see a flyer on the windshield for a band called the Hollows. I know immediately that it's Lola's band. It's the name she and Hiroko picked out years ago when it existed only in their imaginations. Meanwhile, they wrote their own songs and practiced in Lola's grandmother's garage.

I study the flyer while Rose packs the shopping bags into the car. There's a picture of the two of them at a bus stop, waiting with Lola's bass and all Hiroko's percussion instruments. 'Old friends,' I tell Rose.

'Old friends write,' a voice says, and I look up and Lola's standing there.

It's not all that surprising since she lives close by, and she's obviously in the parking lot putting band flyers under windshield wipers. It feels like a small miracle, though, as if she's slipped through the air from the past: short and curvy, long brown hair and olive skin. I want to hug her, but if I do that I might spill everything and cry right here in the parking lot.

'It's been too long,' I say to fill the silence.

'Way too long,' she says, twisting an earring that looks, in the dimness of the parking lot, like a small nail. 'You haven't written for so long we thought you might be dead.'

'I'd have told you,' I say. 'If I was dead.'

She doesn't smile, but she stops twisting the nail. If I told her about Cal, she'd forgive me immediately, but she'd feel guilty when there's nothing for her to feel guilty about. Plus, it doesn't feel right to blurt it out while Rose is packing toilet paper into the car.

'Year 12 sort of took over everything,' I say.

She steps forward and touches my hair, as if she's just noticed that it's cut and bleached now. Her eyes roam all over me, over my black T-shirt and jeans, my skinny frame. She's in a short silver dress, and I try not to look as faded as I feel.

'You don't like it?' I ask, running my hand over my hair.

'I like it,' she says.

'Are you forgiving me?'

She takes the flyer from me, scribbles her phone number on it, and tells me they're playing tonight at a place called Laundry. 'Henry'll be there, and if you're *really* sorry, you'll come anyway,' she says before I can say anything about not wanting to see Henry. 'Be there and all is forgiven.'

I tell Rose about Lola and Hiroko as we leave the parking lot. Lola's on vocals and guitar. Hiroko plays percussion, the glockenspiel, and some other instruments I can't name. As I tell her, I can see the two of them in class, passing notes with lyrics written on them while the teacher isn't looking.

I put the flyer in my pocket. I miss Lola and I don't want her to hate me, but there's no way I'm turning up at Laundry tonight. Life's depressing enough without seeing Henry and Amy holding hands and kissing.

'Speaking of old school friends,' Rose says, 'I bumped into Sophia the other day – you know, your friend Henry's mum. It was good timing too. I'd just found out that the job I got you at the hospital fell through, and when I mentioned it to her, she offered you a job at Howling Books instead.'

Rose is speaking quickly, so it takes me a little while to absorb what she's saying and then think through what this means. Working next to Henry for eight awkward hours a day. Even if we work different shifts, there'll be no avoiding him. He's always in the bookstore. He sleeps in the bookstore. He'll be lying on the fiction couch talking constantly about Amy. He'll be talking to Amy. I imagine her lying on the fiction couch with him.

'No.'

'No?'

'No,' I say again, more forcefully. 'Thanks, but no thanks. Tell Sophia I found another job.'

'Have you found another job?'

'Obviously not.'

'Then you're taking this one. You start at ten, tomorrow morning. Sophia said she was looking for someone with people and computer skills, and that describes you perfectly.'

'I no longer have people skills.'

'This is true, but I chose not to share that with her. I didn't share anything else, either. They don't know about Cal. They don't know you failed Year 12. They think you're taking a year off before college. All they need is someone to create a database and catalog the stock. You can do that, right?'

I can do it, I admit. I just don't want to do it.

I don't want to explain the humiliating situation with Henry, but since I don't have a choice I tell her about liking him, about the last night of the world, Amy, the letter, my declaration of love, him ignoring my declaration of love. Any other human would understand why I couldn't take that job.

But Rose is not like any other human.

'You'll just have to get over it. You want to hide. You *want* to be miserable, but that's not happening. You're taking the job at Howling Books. You're not spending even one day lying on your bed staring at the ceiling.' She looks over at me and then back to the road. 'You have to start living again sometime.'

We take the groceries inside without talking. I'm more determined with every bag that I'm not working with Henry.

'I'd rather be a janitor and clean bathrooms. Let me clean bathrooms. I beg you. Let me be a cleaner at the hospital.'

'You still like him,' Rose says.

'I don't still like him. I don't like anyone.'

Maybe some people have loads of sex to get over their grief, but that didn't happen to me. I broke up with Joel. I haven't kissed anyone since the funeral. I don't want to kiss anyone. I don't want to *see* anyone kiss anyone. I definitely don't want to see Henry and Amy kiss.

'This is my condition for you living here,' Rose says. 'You get up every morning; you go to work. You either do that, or I enroll you in Year 12 again. You're eighteen, so you can decide what to do. You can stay here and do what I say, or you can go home. I don't mean it to sound brutal, but we're all just so fucking *worried* about you.'

I go into the bathroom and shut the door, because it's the only door to shut. I stand looking at myself in the mirror. I'm someone I recognize but don't. I cut off my long hair about a week after the funeral. It was a strange night. I look back and the thing I remember about it is the sky. I hadn't seen one like it before. Flat and starless, as though the world had become a box with a lid on it. I couldn't sleep. I sat on the balcony, staring up for a long time, knowing there were planets and stars and galaxies, but not believing in them anymore.

I like there being a line between the Rachel I was before Cal died – the girl with long blond hair, the scientist, the girl who wore dresses because it was easier to strip down to the swimsuits underneath – and the Rachel with cropped hair, the one who doesn't wear swimsuits anymore and doesn't care what she looks like.

'I just want you to be *you* again,' Rose says, tapping her nails on the door and calling my name to entice me out of the bathroom. 'Do you remember that day?' she says, and I know what day she means without her naming a date or a place or a time. She starts to describe it, and I want her to stop, but I don't want to make a big deal about it. Nothing much and everything happened on that day.

Rose had come to visit in the summer before I started Year 12. She'd arrived home from Chile, turned up in the early morning the way she usually did, appearing in the kitchen with coffee and croissants and the papers. It was summer. Hot by first light.

We ate on the balcony, and Rose told us she'd visited Cape Horn, the land at the southern end of the Tierra del Fuego archipelago. Beyond that are the South Shetland Islands of Antarctica, separated by the Drake Passage. 'The connecting point between the Atlantic and Pacific Oceans,' Cal said, reading from the screen of his phone, pushing up his glasses with his knuckles, scrolling through more information. While he read, Rose put her feet up on the balcony and said, 'First trip. Wherever you go, separately or together, wherever it is, I'll fund it.'

Rose didn't make promises she didn't intend to keep. Cal and I started planning. We'd go together, that much we were certain about. I'd wait till he finished Year 12. The hard part was deciding where.

'The offer still stands,' Rose says tonight. 'Pick a place.'

I pick the past.

The bathroom is too small. Rose keeps tapping. The strange girl stares from the mirror. I think about driving and how good the air will feel from an open window. I unlock the door and come out.

'Can we at least talk about it?' she asks, and I tell her sure, we can talk.

'But tomorrow. I think I'll go see Lola's band tonight.'

I take the flyer, and Rose gives me a spare key to the warehouse. She looks worried, so I kiss her on the cheek. 'Relax. You got through to me. I'm living again.'

This would have been enough for Mum, but Rose isn't Mum.

'I'm not an idiot. You'll drive around all night just to avoid talking.'

That is exactly the plan. 'That is not the plan.'

It feels like we're about to start another fight, but instead Rose relaxes and leans against the counter. 'OK then.' She picks up an apple and bites into it. 'Take a picture of Lola onstage and send it. Show me this proof of life.'

Too smart for her own good is how Gran describes Rose: too adventurous, too honest, too unconventional, too loud. These are the qualities I've always loved about Rose. Until now, when they're working against me.

I drive around to old places while I decide on a plan. Everything seems the same: the streets, the shops, the houses. I pass Gracetown High, where Mum taught science and I went to school. Cal went to a private school across town that had a good music program; he played the piano.

I park outside our old place on Matthews Street, a three-bedroom Californian bungalow, painted cream. Whoever lives there now has kept our chairs out front and the plants, but there are different bikes leaning against the side and different cars in the driveway.

The back of the house was glass when we lived there. I remember Cal and me sitting in the living room one night when a summer storm started. The outside light lit up the rain and the lightning started. Cal and I both loved storms. We loved the accumulation of charge in the air, electricity building in the clouds above and on the earth's surface, moving toward each other.

Cal was interested in science, and he was good at it, but he didn't love it, not the way that I did. He liked science because of all the possibilities, but he believed in other things like time travel and the supernatural. I remember once we watched *Being Human* together, and we had this argument about whether ghosts existed.

Cal thought they did. I thought they didn't. Mum explained to both of us why, according to the second law of thermodynamics, they couldn't exist. Cal chose to believe in them anyway.

I was with Mum. Humans are a highly ordered system, and once we're disordered beyond repair, we don't reorder.

At the funeral, though, after everyone had left the chapel, I stayed. I was waiting for Cal's ghost. I still didn't believe in them, but I had this crazy idea that because he did, they might be possible. 'See, Rach, I'm here,' I imagined him saying as he held up his arms to show the sunlight shining through. Ghosts are nothing but dust and imagination, though, and eventually the funeral director gently told me I had to leave. There was another funeral starting soon.

I think about Rose's ultimatum. Stay here or go home. Cal's everywhere, but at least in the city he was alive. I don't want to go home. I don't think I ever want to go back there.

I take out the flyer and study it. I haven't heard of Laundry, but it's on High Street, not far from here. Going by number, I'd say it was opposite Howling Books. I don't want to see Henry, but the club will be dark, so the chances of running into him are small.

I start the car.

Pride and Prejudice and Zombies

by Jane Austen and Seth Grahame-Smith

Letters left between pp. 44 and 45
December 8–December 11, 2012

> *OK, Pytheas, I'll write back, but only because I feel sorry for you. What kind of guy likes freaks?*
>
> *I'll tell you about me, but first I have some questions for you. Who is Pytheas? Have we spoken before? Why do I never see you putting letters into the book? I've been watching very closely.*
>
> George

> *Dear George,*
>
> *Are you always this suspicious? I don't mind, but I wonder if you trust anyone. You're always on your own at school. I asked to sit at your table at the cafeteria once. You looked at me, said sure, and then got up and walked away. Not exactly welcoming.*

So, Pytheas – I'm glad you asked. He lived in the fourth century, and he was the first person (at least on record) to write about the midnight sun. He's the first known scientific visitor to the Arctic, and he was the first person to record that the moon causes the tides.

You never see me putting letters into the book because I'm incredibly stealthy. ☺

Pytheas

P.S. I saw that you marked the United States on the map – I'd like to go there too. My sister and I would like to dive off the coast of California someday.

OK, Pytheas: things about me.

I like the bookshop. I read a lot. Some favorites are Hugh Howey, Kurt Vonnegut, Ursula K. Le Guin, Margaret Atwood, John Green, Tolstoy (just read Anna Karenina), J. K. Rowling, Philip Pullman, Kirsty Eagar, Melina Marchetta, Charlotte Brontë and Donna Tartt. Lately (you know this), I'm getting into the mash-ups of the classics (Sense and Sensibility and Sea Monsters, that kind of thing).

I like dumplings. My birthday is the first day of winter; I actually like being cold (everywhere except my feet). Music-wise, I like the Finches, Jane's Addiction, Amber Coffman and Wish.

I tend to keep to myself at school because everyone

there seems different from me, and I can't quite find a group I fit with, so I've stopped trying.

I'm sorry about that day in the cafeteria. I don't remember it. But if I'd known you were you, then I would have hung around.

George

Dear George,

Thank you. I accept your apology. If I ever get the courage to walk up to you again, I'll be expecting a warmer reception.

I understand. I changed schools too – but I've made a good friend at our school, so it's bearable. I think you'd like my friend, I know he'd like you. You're in his English class, and he thinks you're interesting. He liked the book report you gave on Liar. He told me you said fuck and didn't realize it.

I haven't heard of those bands, but I downloaded some of their music. I like Wish. They sound kind of dream-like. Have you heard of the Dandy Warhols? I think you might like them.

I read a lot of fiction and I like comics, but I love nonfiction. Like I said, I'm into time theories. I've been reading a lot about the growing block universe. I don't entirely understand the theory, but I like trying to get my head around it.

Pytheas

P.S. I do like freaks, but I don't think you're one. Or if you are, it's in the best possible way. You're gorgeous. (I'll never tell you who I am now.) I like the blue stripe in your hair and I like how you give answers in class and don't care what people say. I like how you're always reading interesting stuff and how you work in a bookstore.

P.P.S. I've left a book in the Letter Library for you. It's one of mine, so you can keep it - Mark Laita's Sea. It's one of my all-time favorite books. I've marked the North Pacific octopus. It can change its appearance and texture to look like even the most intricately patterned coral. It lives about four years, which is longer than other species, and it grows to about five meters long. I'd like to travel to Alaska someday to see one.

Dear Pytheas,

So I read up on the theories of time you mentioned. If the past actually exists, then why can't we travel there? According to the growing block universe theory, wouldn't I still exist in the past? So while I'm here in the present, I'm also there? That makes NO sense, Pytheas.

Thank you for the book. It's very beautiful. Are the photographs enhanced? The fish seem unbelievably bright.

I've been looking at the pictures in almost complete darkness - just with a small flashlight to highlight the fish. I feel like I'm underwater. Have you done that?

The giant octopus is amazing, sure. But my favorite photograph is of the jellyfish. I go to the aquarium sometimes to watch them. They look like ghosts in the water.

Thanks for all the compliments you're giving me - I'd give some back, but I don't know you. Lately I'm distracted in class, because I can't stop wondering who you are. You don't seem like you're one of the popular kids - I mean that in the nicest possible way.

Are you ever planning on telling me who you are? Or will we keep writing like this forever?

George

Dear George,

I thought it might be getting weird that I'm at school and you don't know who I am. But I just can't tell you. I'm worried that if you knew, it might change things and I don't want to stop writing.

The growing block universe does mess with your idea of time, doesn't it? Think about it like this - the universe is growing, and as it grows, slices of space-time are added to it. As slices are added, you move in a forward direction. Travel to the past is impossible, though. Space-time moves in one direction - forward.

Pytheas

Henry

Our hours at Howling Books are flexible. We're open by ten in the morning, and we stay open till at least five, but usually we'll stay open later. We'll almost always open up for a late-night book emergency.

We always close before eight on Fridays, though, because that's when we have our family dinner at Shanghai Dumplings. I'm bringing in the rolling shelves we keep on the street, getting ready to close, when Lola walks in and says she's just seen Rachel.

I don't need to ask her which Rachel she's talking about. There's only one Rachel. *The* Rachel. Rachel Sweetie. My best friend who moved away three years ago and got so busy she forgot all about me.

After she left, I wrote her letters – *long* letters – telling her all the news about the bookshop. I wrote about George and Mum and Dad and Lola and Amy. She sent me one-paragraph letters back, and then the letters turned into one-paragraph emails, and then she put me on group emails, and then she stopped writing to me altogether.

'She's ignoring me,' I'd say to Lola, looking at the long emails she was getting from Rachel. 'Has she said anything to you?' I asked, and she shook her head. Lola is a shit liar. Rachel had said something to her but Lola was too loyal to tell me, so I was left to wonder.

'She's cut her hair short, and bleached it,' Lola says, and now I'm trying to picture her and I don't want to do that. I don't want to wonder what she's doing.

I make a face to let her know that Rachel has nothing to do with me. 'I still don't know why we stopped being friends, but we did, so I don't want to catch up with her.'

Lola turns her back to the counter and hauls herself up on it so she's near the mint bowl. She takes one and says, 'You need to get over it. She's back and I want to hang out.'

'I'm over it. I'm completely over it. I'm over that she wrote to you and not to me. Completely over that she wouldn't take my phone calls. More than completely over that she left town without saying good-bye.'

'The way I heard it, you texted and told her you'd slept in.'

'Is that why she's angry? Because I *always* sleep in. I've slept in almost every day of my life and Rachel knows that. She could have driven past here on her way out of town, woke me up, and said good-bye.'

'You do really seem to be over it,' Lola says.

'But you know what she did instead? She sent me a text saying that my copy of *American Gods* was on the front steps of her house. It rained before I got there. It was totally ruined.'

Lola takes another mint. 'Lucky you work in a bookstore and

you have five other copies on the shelf and two in your personal collection.'

'Not the point,' I say.

She passes me a flyer. 'The Hollows are playing tonight at Laundry. Which is, for your convenience, just across the road.'

Lola and Hiroko have been playing together officially as the Hollows since the Year 11 formal. Unofficially they've been dreaming of a band since Year 8. They're a little like Arcade Fire meets the Go-Betweens meets Caribou, and they're good. Lola made a deal with the owner of Laundry that they can play on Friday nights for an hour before the main band comes on. Until she earns enough from the bass to pay the rent, she supports herself by working at the local supermarket and filling in at the bookshop if anyone's sick.

I tell her I'll be there as she slides off the counter.

'Full disclosure: I asked Rachel,' she says. 'You should come and patch things up with her.'

Something tells me patching up will not be a possibility. You can't patch up someone forgetting about you. For the rest of your life you'll always be wondering if they'll forget about you again. You'll always know that they'd be a hundred per cent fine without you but you wouldn't be a hundred per cent fine without them.

I lock up after Lola's gone and head to Shanghai Dumplings. On the way I distract myself from Rachel by thinking about Amy. I've had my phone on silent all day and deliberately not checked, because it's a truth universally acknowledged that a watched phone never rings, especially when you're waiting on a text from your ex-girlfriend explaining why she doesn't love you anymore.

She has rung. There's a missed call, but no message.

I'm thinking about whether I should dial the number and

see, when I walk into Greg Smith. I'm looking down, and he's standing in my way, so my shoulder knocks into his. I ignore him and keep walking. Greg Smith was in my class at school, and every time I see him it makes me question the universe. He's a complete idiot, but he's got supernaturally white teeth and perfect hair. Why reward the idiots? Surely, if you don't want them to win, don't make them good-looking.

'Heard Amy dumped your arse,' he says when I've walked a few steps past him. I find it's best not to engage with Greg, but every time, I engage anyway. I engage when he calls my sister weird. I engage when he calls me weird. I engage when he calls Lola a lesbian like there's something wrong with that. I engage when he says that poetry is stupid. I'm willing to admit that some poetry is stupid. If Greg wrote poetry, it would be stupid. But Pablo Neruda, William Blake and Emily Dickinson, just to name a few, are the furthest thing from stupid that words can get.

'She didn't dump me, actually. We're still together. Flying out on the twelfth of March,' I say, and keep walking before he can say anything else. He'll find out sooner or later I was lying, but it'll be sometime that I'm not standing right in front of him. One of the great things about finishing high school is that you can finally get away from the dickheads.

I'm only in a bad mood till I walk into the restaurant. Mum, Dad, George and I have been coming to Shanghai Dumplings every Friday, except for the Fridays when we host book club, for as long as I can remember. We always get the pork dumplings, the pan-fried dumplings, the wontons with hot chili sauce, the salt-and-pepper squid, the prawns and greens and spring rolls.

Since Mum left, we've kept up the tradition. She's moved out of the bookshop, but she still comes to dumplings, and for an hour at least we're a family again, and that feels good. Weird and sad, but good.

Mai Li's working the door, the same as always. Her family owns the place. I know her from school. She's studying journalism this year, but her main love is performance poetry, which she writes on her phone while she's walking around. I can't work out if she speaks like performance poetry, or that's just the way I hear her.

'How be life, Henry?' she asks, and I tell her, 'Life be shit, Mai Li.'

'Shit, why?'

'Shit because Amy dumped me.'

She stops handing out menus to customers and gives the news the pause it deserves. 'Life be fucked then, Henry,' she says, and hands me a menu. 'I think they're fighting.'

'Really?'

'No one's eating. They've been yelling,' she says, and I start climbing the stairs.

Mum and Dad don't yell. They're the kind of people who quote literature and try to talk about everything. Even when Mum was leaving, they didn't yell. The silence in the bookshop was so loud George and I went next door to Frank's to get away from it, but even when we were gone, they fought in silence.

I get to the table and George is in her usual seat next to Dad. I take my seat next to Mum. Based on the worried look George gives me, I'm pretty sure Mai Li was right.

Usually at Friday-night dinners we talk nonstop about books and the world. Last week we started with George. She'd read *1984* by George Orwell and *The One Safe Place* by Tania Unsworth. She'd started *The Road* by Cormac McCarthy.

The first rule of our family book discussions is you can't spend forever explaining the plot. You get twenty-five words or less for that but endless time for what you thought about it. 'Orwell – a world controlled by the state. Unsworth – set in a world after global warming. McCarthy – father and son surviving in a post-apocalyptic world.'

I asked her what it was about those terrible worlds that fascinated her, and she thought about it for a while. The thing I love about George is that she takes ideas and books and the discussion of those things seriously. 'It's the characters, mostly, not the world. It's how people are when they've lost everything or when it's dangerous to think for themselves.'

The conversation turned to me, and what I'd been reading. *Where Things Come Back* by John Corey Whaley. I took out the book and passed it around. I didn't want to give away too much, so I just told them it was about Cullen Witter, whose brother disappears. The book starts with the narrator describing the first dead body he'd ever seen, and after that opening, I couldn't stop reading.

Mum talked about Jennifer Egan's *A Visit from the Goon Squad,* and she looked kind of sad when she explained to George and me that time is the goon, that it pushes us around. George had to look up *goon* to find out it meant a kind of gang member. Dad had read the book. He looked kind of sad, too, and it occurred to me that maybe love is the goon that pushes us around. 'Maybe,' Dad said when I mentioned it to him later. 'But I like to think of love as being slightly more forgiving than time.'

Tonight it's a whole different thing. There's no book talking. Dad's stabbing a prawn dumpling straight through the middle. 'We need to talk to you,' Mum says, which is the same way she brought up the divorce. 'We need to talk to you' is never good news.

'Your mother really thinks we should sell the shop,' Dad says, and it's pretty clear it's something he doesn't want to do.

'You know, there are people making serious offers on the building. Life would be a lot easier for all of us if we sold,' Mum says. 'We're talking substantial money.'

'Do we need substantial money?' Dad asks.

'Secondhand books aren't exactly a thriving industry,' Mum says. 'What were the takings today, Henry?'

I put a whole dumpling in my mouth to avoid answering.

No, they're not thriving and they probably won't thrive again. Like Amy says all the time: *Wake up and smell the internet, Henry.* But does that mean we should sell? I don't know.

The thing about our family, though, is we all get a vote, so Mum and Dad aren't going to make decisions without us. George is staring at her plate with ferocious intensity, like she's hoping she can make it into a portal and disappear. I'm guessing she hasn't cast her vote yet. She plays Scrabble with Dad every night, and she loves reading in the window with Ray Bradbury. But she misses Mum so much I've heard her crying in her room. She'll vote with me, because she doesn't want to take sides. That makes mine the deciding vote.

'Do you want to work in the bookstore till it dies, Henry?' Mum asks, and Dad says he doesn't think that's a fair question, and she says he's free to make a counter-argument, and he says, 'If we all gave up on the things we love when it gets hard, it'd be a terrible world.' It feels like we're talking about more than books, here, which is why George is voting with me.

I try to see into the future – twenty years, say – and I know it's unlikely we're still making a go of it. I see myself sitting behind the counter reading Dickens in Dad's spot, talking to Frieda, the sun coming in the window and lighting up universes of dust and the relics that are secondhand books. I see myself going off at night to work a second job to pay the bills, like Dad's had to do a couple of times over the years. Eventually I see a world without books, definitely without secondhand bookstores. I have a flashback to Amy and me talking about the bookshop when she loaned me money to pay for travel insurance. 'If you want to have a life, Henry, you need to get a proper job.'

'How bad is it?' I ask Mum. She does the books. She's the practical one who thinks about the future.

'It's bad, Henry. We barely make ends meet. I want to be able to pay for George's college fees next year. I want to retire someday. I want to leave you and George with a future.'

And suddenly it's a no-brainer why Amy broke up with me. I'm destined to be unemployed. She's destined to be a lawyer. At the moment, my plan is to live with my dad and my sister long-term. Her plan is to buy her own flat. The reason she broke up with me can't be as simple as that, but it must have something to do with it. I hardly ever have money to take her out.

I love secondhand books; I love books. But if things are as bad as Mum says, then selling's the best thing for all of us. 'If there's a huge offer on the table, maybe we should think about it,' I say, avoiding Dad's eyes.

There's a sad quiet after I say that, and I almost take it back.

'Maybe we should just talk to the agents,' Mum says, and because no one argues, it feels like an agreement to do that.

George goes to the bathroom, mainly to avoid the discussion.

While she's gone, Mum tells me she's hired a couple of people to catalog the books so we can tell what stock we have. 'You know one of them, in fact – Rachel.'

I don't have to ask her which Rachel. Again, there's only one Rachel.

'I saw her aunt in the supermarket last week. She told me that Rachel was moving back to the city, but the job Rose lined up for her fell through. Rachel's good with computers, so I told Rose she could have the job.'

I listen to Mum and try to imagine the conditions that would have to exist for Rachel to accept a job working with me at Howling Books. Maybe she suffered a blow to the head and she's got amnesia.

I don't respond. I'm guessing I look unimpressed, though, because she says, 'I thought you were best friends?'

'That was before she moved,' I say. 'We haven't spoken in years.'

'Should I un-hire her?' she asks. 'I don't think I can un-hire her.'

I'd be lying if I said I didn't want to see Rachel. I've missed her. And if she's taken the job, then maybe she wants to see me. 'Don't un-hire her,' I say as George comes back and says she's not hungry anymore and wants to go home.

Mum leaves with her, so it's just Dad and me, at the table with too many dumplings and a whole heap of quiet. 'You're disappointed in me,' I say. 'I haven't officially cast my vote yet.'

'We all have a vote, Henry. We're all part of the decision. Don't look so worried.' He puts his hand on my shoulder. 'I'm not disappointed in you.'

'I read an article that said secondhand books will be relics eventually,' I tell him, still trying to make excuses for how things went tonight.

'Do you know what the word *relic* actually means, the dictionary definition?' he asks, offering me the prawn crackers.

I take one, and tell him I don't know.

'It means "sacred",' he says. 'As in the bones of saints.'

The Great Gatsby

by F. Scott Fitzgerald

Letter found between pp. 8 and 9

To my love,

If I knew where you were, I would post this letter. But I don't, so I will have to leave it here. I know how you love F Scott. More than you love me, I think. I searched the bookshelves. I feel certain you've taken our copy. We bought it together. Don't you remember? So it wasn't really yours to take.

I got your letter. It was better than a text, I suppose, but you're wrong. It wasn't the kinder way to end things. It would have hurt just the same if you'd said good-bye to my face, but it would have stung less.

Where have you gone, my love? After ten years I think knowing this is more than my due. Write me one line to let me know where you are. So that I do not wonder, for the rest of our lives when I imagine you, what the background is to your face.

John

Henry

I walk back from the restaurant toward Laundry, thinking about the bones of saints and Rachel and whether or not I should vote to sell. The problem with the bookshop is that selling makes sense. Mum made a good argument, and she's always been the practical one in the family.

The problem with Rachel is what I should say when I see her. I don't know if I can be her friend again if she doesn't say that she missed me or give me a good explanation for why she never wrote. I don't have a whole lot of dignity, but I've got some.

I'm worrying about this when I walk straight into her. I don't even see her. We collide on the street, and I'm in the middle of saying sorry before I realize that it's her.

The first thing I think is: thank God she's back. The second think I think is: she's grown up gorgeous. She always was gorgeous, of course, but she's grown up even more gorgeous than I thought she would. There's something different about her, a change I can't pinpoint, and I can't stop my eyes from roaming all over her, checking out the changes – her hair's short now, like Lola said, and bleached. She's wearing an old black T-shirt and jeans. She's taller, or maybe it's just that she's so thin, or maybe it's both.

'Hi,' I say.

'Hi,' she says, and then looks away, like she barely recognizes me.

'*Henry,*' I say. 'Henry Jones. Best friend for seven years. Ringing any bells?'

'I know,' she says, still not really looking at me.

She takes a flyer out of her pocket and unfolds it. 'I'm here for Lola,' she says, and I can't help feeling the end of that sentence is 'not you'.

'Me too,' I say. 'Yep. I'm here for Lola. Who is,' I tell her, 'my best friend now, since my other best friend left town and forgot all about me.' I scuff at the ground. 'How much time does it take to write a letter?'

'I wrote letters,' she says.

'Yeah, thanks for those paragraphs with basically nothing in them.'

'You're welcome,' she says, and points over my shoulder. 'The line's moving.'

We pay our money and get our wrists stamped. Laundry's set up in the shell of an old laundromat: the machines are spread around the bar, and in some corners you can still smell cheap detergent and half-dried sheets. It's small, so I'm not following Rachel; I'm walking behind her to the bar. Still, she turns back to look at me like I'm a stalker.

I don't understand. I've missed her. Even now, when she's not being herself, I miss her. 'How can you not have missed me? How is that possible?'

For a second I think she's about to admit that she did. She almost smiles. But then she says, 'It's a complete mystery.'

'You were about to admit it. You were about to say, "I missed you so much I cried at night. I kissed your photograph daily."'

'I didn't take your photograph with me,' she says, and points across the room to an empty table. 'Look. I see some friends.'

I'm watching her sit alone in preference to talking to me when Lola comes up beside me. 'Have you seen her?' she asks.

'Yes,' I say. 'And she was very rude. Nothing like her old self.'

'She was always kind of rude.'

'No, she wasn't. She was funny and smart and loyal. A little over-organized, sure, with all those notes she took in class, and the way she alphabetized the books in her locker, but everyone's got something and it worked in my favor over the years. I still have the notes she took for me when I was sick that time. Everything neatly labeled—'

'Who are you talking about?' Lola asks, cutting me off.

I point over to the table, where no one's sitting anymore. I wonder whether I imagined her. 'Rachel.'

'I'm talking about Amy,' she says, and I notice she seems worried. 'I have bad news.'

'How bad?' I ask.

'*Bad,* bad,' she says. 'Really bad. I'm talking *extreme* badness.'

When Lola fell out of a tree in Year 5, and we asked if she was hurt, she said, 'A little, I guess.' She'd broken her leg in three places. It's in her nature to play things down.

'All I ask is that you make it quick and merciful,' I say.

She closes her eyes and tells me, 'AmyiswithGregSmith.'

Because of the way it's all crammed in together, it takes me a while to separate the words.

'Amy's with Greg Smith?' I repeat when they're finally separate and in my ears. 'And by *with,* you mean . . . ?'

'Holding hands, kissing. They're on the other side of the bar.'

The information just doesn't compute. Greg Smith is the kind of guy who thinks it's funny to steal a guy's clothes and towel after swimming and then post a picture of him on Facebook while he stands there naked, asking a teacher for clothes. Amy couldn't like Greg Smith.

'How do you feel?' Lola asks.

'Like I've just had every single one of my organs harvested while I'm still alive.'

'Good to know you're not overreacting,' she says. 'I have to go play. Don't get drunk.' She points a finger at me. 'My love for you is unconditional, but you're an idiot when you drink.'

It's true. Her love for me *is* unconditional, and I *am* a total idiot when I drink. But if there was ever an occasion to be a total idiot, this is it.

It's a truth universally acknowledged, according to George, that shit days get shitter. Shit nights roll into shit mornings that roll into shit afternoons and back into shit, starless midnights. Shitness, my sister says, has a momentum that good luck just doesn't have.

I push my way through the crowd to the bar to order a drink. By chance, Rachel is standing there when I arrive. I'm hoping I look so pitiful that she'll feel sorry for me and end this stupid fight. 'I'm having a bad week,' I say. 'I'm talking extreme badness.'

'Not interested, Henry,' she says, and walks away in the direction of the stage.

'Is that the girl?' Katia, the bartender, asks.

I tutored Katia in English the year Rachel left, so she knows all about us. 'That is Rachel. My ex-best friend.'

'The one you secretly love.'

'I don't secretly love her.'

'You don't talk about a girl as much as you talked about Rachel if you don't secretly love her.'

'I love her. I'm just not *in* love with her,' I say, and drink my beer fast. At the moment I would like nothing more than to be a bystander in my life: observing the badness but not feeling it. I order another beer and another because the blur under my skin feels more than good. It feels great.

Until I turn to my left and see Amy and Greg sitting side by side on the laundromat's old locked-together plastic chairs, holding hands. She seems so happy. She's laughing and looking at him the way she looked at me that first night. Completely focused. Laughing. Leaning close. She looks gorgeous: red hair falling loose over a long green dress.

He looks gorgeous, too, the fucker. The lights are picking up and reflecting the whiteness of his teeth and making his hair look extra shiny. I see myself in the mirror that runs along the back of the bar. My hair is doing that defeated thing and my teeth are the white of an average person. I'm in the clothes I've been wearing for the last couple of days – my Bukowski *Love Is a Dog from Hell* T-shirt, and jeans.

'Look at them,' I say to Katia.

'Shakespeare,' she says, the light from the bar glinting off her pink hair, 'that girl is not for you.'

'She's my soul mate,' I tell her.

'Then I am worried about your soul,' she says, and goes back to serving the other customers.

It's not the first time I've heard Amy wasn't right for me. Obviously Rachel never liked her. George doesn't like the way Amy turns up at the bookshop when she's lonely and then disappears when she's not. But it isn't like that. It's more like she can't stay away from me any more than I can stay away from her. I always took her back. I will always take her back. I might tell myself I won't, but then she shows up at the bookshop and it feels like something that's out of my control. She's my destiny. She's not some total moron's destiny.

I stumble toward them through the crowd, trying all the while to figure out what to say to Amy when I arrive. The words to get her back exist; I just have to work out the order of them.

But I've got nothing. I stand in front of them, staring and swaying for a while. Then I wave across their hands, which are looped together. 'This is so . . . disturbing. He's – it's – *Greg Smith*.'

'Henry,' she says, and he stands without dropping her hand, so she's pulled up with him. They're looped together in front of me, when a week ago Amy and I were looped.

'I don't understand. He's a complete idiot. Look at him.'

But as I say it, *I* look at him. I take a good long look at Greg Smith. He's handsome. He's well dressed; he wouldn't have had to borrow the last hundred dollars from his girlfriend to buy his round-the-world ticket. I bet he's paid for her drink. He's going to college. He's studying law. He's got a life plan to go with his white teeth.

I think about a lot of things, standing here. I think about how Amy probably hates making out on the floor of the bookshop;

that I intend to live there indefinitely with my dad and George. To live there with them always, really, because it's their bookshop too. And then I have a flashback to me dressed in my secondhand suit for the formal, picking up Amy in the bookshop van. She said it didn't matter, but maybe it did. Maybe a lot of things I thought didn't matter actually did. Maybe that's why she keeps going away and coming back. She comes back because she can't stop loving me. She leaves because I don't have my shit together. I need to get myself together. I need to get a better haircut and a decent life plan.

'We're selling the bookshop,' I tell her. 'I'll be able to move into my own place when we get back.'

'You're not going anywhere,' Greg says.

'I am going somewhere. And, Amy, I want you to come with me.'

Maybe it's the light, but I don't think it is. She looks unsure for a second. One second of uncertainty tells me all I need to know. I can have her back if I change.

Greg nudges me then, just gently, just enough, and I fall backward into a crowd that instinctively clears a space for me. I look up from my position on the floor at Amy, and she looks back down at me sadly. In those eyes I read something. I read that she wants me to change. If you change, her eyes are saying, I'll come back.

I close my eyes to get some balance, and I feel hands pulling me up. I think it's her, helping me, but when I open my eyes, it's Rachel. 'You want her back?' she says. 'Then get up and stop being so pathetic.'

Rachel

I'm definitely not in love with Henry anymore, and it's a relief. He smells the same – peppermint and cedar and a hint of old books. He sounds the same – gentle and funny. But I don't get that feeling. I don't think about kissing him. I'm not fixated on his hair. I'm cured.

You're having a really bad week? I think as I walk away from the bar, through the crowd, toward the stage. A really bad week ends in death, Henry. I don't know what's happened to you this week, but unless it involves death, it's really not that bad.

Lola and Hiroko are onstage. I focus on them to take my mind off Henry. They're playing a cover of Cat Power's 'Good Woman'. Lola played it for me once before, in her grandmother's garage. She's even better than I remember. I take a photo and send it to Rose. I send it to Mum as well, trying not to think about how she'll be alone on the beach. I turn off my phone and get lost in the music. I yell with the crowd when Lola does her solo. I move as close as I can to the speakers so thought is impossible.

The set ends and Lola and Hiroko climb down from the stage. Lola takes my water bottle, drinks from it, and hands it back.

'Thank you,' I tell her.

'You're welcome,' she says, and then turns to point through the club toward the bar. 'Henry's drinking.'

'He's having a bad week,' I tell her.

'Amy dumped him and now they're not going overseas and she's here somewhere with Greg Smith.'

'Amy dumped him?' I ask.

'Amy's always dumping him,' Hiroko says, and Lola confirms it's a regular occurrence.

'We've got more sets to play,' Lola says, 'so I need you to look after him. If you still want me to forgive you, that is.' She points across the room.

I walk back to the bar, but by the time I get there, Henry's gone. I finally see him stumbling toward Amy and Greg.

'I think Shakespeare might need some help,' the girl behind the bar says, and puts out her hand. 'I'm Katia.'

'Rachel,' I say.

'I know. Shakespeare told me all about how much he missed you,' she says, opening and closing her hands to imitate Henry's mouth going on and on about me.

I like the thought of Henry missing me. I like the thought of him telling Katia he misses me. 'Amy's no good for him,' Katia says as we watch Henry rambling away in front of her. 'He's a nice guy. He tutored me for free a while back.'

Henry is a nice guy. He might be hopelessly in love with a girl I don't like all that much. He might have been a coward three years ago. But apart from not knowing what to do when I confessed my love for him, he's never actually let me down.

Greg pushes him. It's more of a tap really, but it's enough to send Henry backward to the floor. Amy stares at him but doesn't help. Get up, I think. Get up and walk away. He doesn't. I don't think he can. He's too unsteady on his feet.

Before I can change my mind, I walk across and try to heave him up. He's too heavy and he's not helping himself. I try again, but he doesn't move. Greg and his friends are laughing, so I lean in and say quietly so only he can hear, 'You want her back? Then get up and stop being so pathetic.'

He frowns, but he puts his arm around my shoulder and pushes himself up. I help him to a chair, but he's not in a state to walk, so I look around for someone to help carry him home. Lola and Hiroko still have a couple of sets to play before they're done. I'm not asking Amy.

I've decided to ignore her. It's been a long time since the conversation in the bathroom, a long time since Henry chose to spend his last night of the world with her, and a long time since I loved Henry. It's none of my business if he's still making an idiot of himself over her.

But then she says, 'Nice hair, Rachel.'

It has been a long time, but it turns out I do still have some things to say. I leave the hair comment for now, because I couldn't care less what she thinks about the way I look. I skip straight to the point. 'Guys might like you. Many guys might like you, but you're not good enough for Henry. You've never been good enough for Henry.'

'You haven't been here,' she says. 'How would you know?'

I know because anyone good enough for Henry wouldn't leave

him on the floor when he fell down, I think, but all I say is, 'I *know.*' I know because he's a great guy. I'm looking at the best guy, and I'm not looking at the best girl. I'm definitely not looking at the best girl for Henry.

'You still like him,' she says, and it doesn't make me angry like it did three years ago. It doesn't hurt. It doesn't hit home. I don't like him, not that way. 'He's my best friend,' I tell her. 'And I have a job in the bookstore as of today, so from now on I'll be looking out for him.'

I turn around to pick him up and take him home, but he's gone.

I do a few loops of the club, looking for him. Despite my new hair, some people from school recognize me and I get caught talking to them. Emily, Aziza and Beth want to know what I'm studying. I don't admit to failing because that will inevitably lead to the bigger story that I don't want to tell. And even if I did end up telling it, I wouldn't want to be shouting the news about Cal over music in a club. So instead I tell them I'm taking a year off to save some money, but yes, I got into college and I'm going to major in marine biology. Their lives have gone as planned – Emily's studying the stars, Aziza's interested in environmental law and Beth is doing science and thinking about pre-med.

Before the conversation can go any further, I say, 'I'm looking for Henry. He's pretty drunk and he needs help. Have you seen him?' They haven't, so I keep moving. I walk fast, avoiding people I recognize and people who look twice at me.

After about half an hour I give up, thinking he must have stumbled home, when I find him. I'm in the girls' toilets, washing my hands, and I hear drunken poetry being recited from the end stall.

I walk down to it, push open the door, and there he is, lying on the ground, his head between the wall and the bowl. 'Do you mind? I'm having a private moment here, Rachel.'

I crouch on the floor beside him. 'Here's a tip for a private moment: don't have it on the floor of the girls' toilets.'

'The girls'?' he asks.

'The added extras didn't give it away?'

He lifts his head and squints at the unit in the opposite corner. 'Not a mailbox?'

'Not a mailbox, Henry,' I say as I try, unsuccessfully, to haul him into a standing position.

'Leave me here. I'm dead.'

'You're not dead, Henry.'

'You're right. Dead would be better than this. Amy is with Greg Smith. The love of my life is, as we speak, kissing a moron.'

'Henry, if the love of your life is kissing a moron, it's probably time to reassess whether or not she's the love of your life.'

He makes a little head movement to indicate I may have a point, and then takes my hand and struggles himself into a standing position. We rest here for a while, holding each other, while he gains his balance.

'You smell like apples,' he says.

'Don't smell me, Henry.'

'Amy always smells, just faintly, of lemon. I could taste it when I kissed her.'

'Don't feel you have to talk. I'm really very comfortable with the quiet,' I tell him as we walk out of the toilets.

. . .

'Sleep it off, Shakespeare,' Katia calls on our way past her, and Henry gives her a wave. I can see what he hasn't noticed: Amy on the other side of the bar, watching the two of us. According to the emails I got from Lola over the years, Henry always looked more attractive to Amy the second he was with someone else.

The night's still warm; the heat's trapped in concrete and sky. Henry's leaning on my shoulder with all his weight, which would have been fine ten months ago when I was fit enough to swim five kilometers in the ocean, but now my arms are aching.

It's Friday night, though, and no clear break in the traffic, so I have to walk us the long way to the bookstore, via the pedestrian lights. Henry talks to every local he sees. He's got quite a lot to say about Amy and The Dickhead. I try pulling him away but there's no moving Henry when he's in the middle of a rant, so when he starts on about Amy to a couple and their Great Dane, I sit on a bench and rest while he gets it all out. His arms spread wide to demonstrate the size of his love for Amy and small to indicate the size of Greg's brain.

'This,' he says, pointing in my direction, 'is my long lost best friend, Rachel Sweetie. Rachel and I haven't spoken in a while,' he says. 'Because she didn't miss me. She left town without waking me up. She left my Gaiman out in the rain.'

Even drunk, Henry's still keeping up the lie.

The couple leaves, and Henry sways across to the bench. He keeps opening and shutting his right eye like he's trying to get a clear picture of me. 'You've come back rude and gorgeous,' he says, and leans his head on my shoulder.

'Not gorgeous,' I say, moving my hand over my hair.

'It makes you look like Audrey Hepburn. If she'd been a surfer.'

'I don't surf.'

'Neither did Audrey Hepburn,' he says, and leaves the bench to lie on the sidewalk. 'I just need to rest a while,' he says as a man walks carefully past to avoid stepping on him.

Henry looks at me and pats the concrete. I think briefly about leaving him there but the thought of going back to Rose's isn't all that appealing, so I lie next to him. His arm touches mine, and I let myself think about how good it is to be with him again.

I never planned on ignoring Henry forever, just until he wrote saying he was sorry, he was flattered, but he didn't feel the same way. As soon as he told the truth, I planned to forgive him.

'Why?' he asks again tonight. 'I mean, we were *best* friends. And I know *for a fact* that you wrote to Lola.' He turns his head to the side so our faces are almost touching. 'Why?'

'Why do you think?'

'You didn't miss me,' he says.

Henry's a terrible liar and even if he wasn't, he's so drunk that the truth is spilling out of him. He's genuinely confused. 'You didn't get the letter,' I say, wondering how that's possible since he looks in the *Prufrock* every day, and even if he didn't, I left him a note in his book.

'What letter?' he asks, and I know that however it happened, however that letter went missing, it went. I think about all the letters he's written me over the last three years. I think about him waiting for my reply, seeing that I'd replied to Lola and not him.

'*What letter?*' he asks again.

I almost tell him. I should tell him, but I stop myself. There's no point now. All it'll do is embarrass both of us. 'It was just a good-bye letter. I left it for you on the counter at the bookstore but I guess it went missing.'

'What did it say?' he asks.

'Good-bye, the way most good-bye letters do, Henry.'

'But why didn't you reply to *my* letters?'

'I got busy. I met a guy called Joel.'

'Was he your best friend?' he asks, and he sounds so hurt.

'I'm so sorry, Henry. I was preoccupied with school and new friends. But I should have written. I'm sorry. I'm really sorry.'

'Did you miss me at all?'

'I did,' I say, and at the same time I tell myself not to do something stupid and cry in front of him. Don't tell him how you ached for him at the funeral. How desperate you were for him to turn up, without being asked, and hold your hand.

'So we're friends again?' he asks, and I tell him we are.

'Good friends,' he says.

'Good friends,' I say, and as proof, which he seems to need, I tell him I'm taking the job at the bookstore.

'Of course you're taking it,' he says. 'For as long as it's there.'

I ask him what he means, and he says tonight he voted to sell the bookstore. 'I sell the shop, I get some money, Amy and I travel, and when we move back, I can afford to rent my own place. No more making out in the self-help section.'

'You make out in the self-help section?' I ask.

'I'll study and become something.'

You're something now, I think. 'Be sure,' I say, and he tells me the one thing he's sure about is Amy.

I know it's time to get up because Henry starts reciting poetry. I get my poetry from two places – school and Henry – so I haven't heard any for a while. The last poem I heard in Henry's voice was

'The Love Song of J. Alfred Prufrock'. Tonight it's one I don't know.

His words drop drunk and heavy, and I see the poem as Henry speaks it. A raining world, a hiding sun, a person fighting to love the terrible days.

'It's "Dark August",' he tells me. 'By Derek Walcott.' The poem's not about Cal, not about a boy drowning, but everything feels as though it's about Cal, now.

'Everything goes to hell; the mountains fume,' Henry says, the words loose and soft because he's tired. *'Don't you know I love you but am hopeless at fixing the rain?'*

'Are you still searching for that book for Frederick?' I ask, and he says he is.

Henry believes in the impossible, the same as Cal did. He thinks he can find that book against all odds.

He recites the poem one more time because I ask him. There's something in it that I need to find. An answer, maybe, to how it's done. How a person starts living again. I don't find it. All the poem does is make me ache, in places unlocatable.

I lose sense of time, lying here with Henry on the sidewalk, the cars moving past. It could be three years ago, when Cal was still alive. 'I need to go home,' I say, but Henry's too drunk for me to explain why that's no longer possible.

There's still a light on inside the bookstore, and it gives the shop a soft glow. I've always loved this place. I loved the polished floorboards and the deep, rich wood of the shelves. I loved the way the spines of the books looked, neatly aligned one next to the other. I loved it because I could always find Henry here.

I ring the bell, and while I wait, I look at the front window. There's the seat where George always sat reading with Ray Bradbury on her knee. The books in the window are a new display – Zadie Smith, Jeffrey Eugenides, Jonathan Safran Foer, Simmone Howell, Fiona Wood, Nam Le – and I've read none of them.

I look closely at the book at the center of the display – *Cloud Atlas* by David Mitchell. It has a pink cover. At the bottom is a small typewriter with paper flying out, the paper turning into clouds as it rises. I can't name what it makes me feel; sadness, maybe, at the pointlessness of an atlas for clouds – at things that move from minute to minute.

Michael comes to the door with Frederick. 'Lucky I was here playing Scrabble,' Frederick says as they take Henry off my hands. I follow with his wallet and keys that have fallen from his pocket.

'My father,' Henry says as they tumble through the door.

'My son,' his dad replies, helping him toward the fiction couch.

He walks back and kisses me on the cheek. 'We've missed you. Henry's missed you.'

'Amy's going out with Greg Smith,' I say to explain why Henry's drunk. 'I found him in the girls' toilets.'

'In my defense, I was too drunk to know it was the girls' toilets,' Henry says from the couch.

'Go to sleep,' his dad tells him. 'It'll seem better in the morning.'

'No offense, Dad,' Henry says, 'but unrequited love is just as shit in the morning as it is at night. Possibly more shit because you have a whole day ahead of you.'

'No offense taken,' Michael says. 'You've got a point there.'

'They should kill the victims of unrequited love,' Henry says. 'They should just take us out the second it happens.'

'That would certainly thin the population,' Michael says, and he tucks a blanket around his son.

Henry calls me over. He beckons while I'm walking toward him, waves and waves and waves till I'm close, and then he waves me down to face level. His breath smells of beer.

'I wish I'd gotten the letter.'

'Forget the letter.'

'OK,' he says. 'But I want you to know something.'

'What?' I ask.

'I *missed* you,' he says, and then he kisses me on the mouth and falls asleep.

I don't like admitting it, but I can feel Henry's kiss all the way home. It was a drunken kiss, a mistaken kiss, and he's so out of it he probably thought he was kissing Amy, and I don't like him anyway, but still, I think about it just the same.

I've parked, and I'm sitting in the car trying to get the energy to move when Rose walks out of the warehouse and gets into the car. 'Are you avoiding me?'

'I'm avoiding myself,' I tell her. 'Sorry about before.'

'Me too,' she says, and takes a small breath. 'So I called Gran. She suggested the value of compromise.'

'Translated: she said you're stubborn and you might try listening once in a while?'

'That's quite close to how the conversation went, yes. I'd do anything for you. Even call my mother,' she says, and shifts around so she's looking at me. 'Want some good news?'

'I would really love some good news.'

'I think I've found you a job cleaning at the hospital.'

'We're in some serious fucking trouble if that's the good news.'

'Don't swear. Gran'll think it came from me.'

'We'll blame Henry. For a guy with a great vocabulary he leans heavily on the word *shit*,' I say. 'Don't think I'm not appreciative of the cleaning job, but I've decided to work at the bookstore.'

'This is why I didn't have kids,' she says, getting out of the car. 'And remember, the offer of travel still stands.'

I lie in bed thinking about tonight, thinking about Henry and the kiss, which leads to thoughts about Joel, the last person whose kiss meant something. We met on the beach, over the black rocks where the sand is flat and unshifting. He was looking in the tide pools, and Cal went over to see what he was doing. They were crouched at the edge for ages, Joel reading the tiny details of the beach – small shells housed in the rough texture of rocks. I knew Joel from school, so I walked over eventually. I could feel his look on my skin. I'd spent years with Henry barely noticing I was a girl, and there I was, visible to someone.

We kissed at a party later that year. Joel smiled and I knew what it meant. We went to a quiet place near the water. The moon was a floating light on the water. We stripped off our clothes and swam right through.

'You can come back,' Joel said on the night we broke up. 'When things get better.'

How long does it take? I wonder before I close my eyes and dream about clouds and unstoppable rain and Henry.

Great Expectations

by Charles Dickens

Written on title page: *Dear Sophia, for you, on the first day of our new life in the bookstore. See page 508, Michael.*

Markings on p. 508

> *Out of my thoughts! You are part of my existence, part of myself.* <u>*You have been in every line I have ever read*</u> *since I first came here, the rough common boy whose poor heart you wounded even then. You have been in every prospect I have ever seen since – on the river, on the sails of the ships, on the marshes, in* <u>*the clouds, in the light, in the darkness, in the wind, in the woods, in the sea, in the streets.*</u>

Letter left between pp. 508 and 509

Michael,

As you're not returning my call about the sale of the bookstore, and you disappear when I stop by, it seems there's no other way to talk but by letter. I hope that I have a better chance of reaching you through this book than the ordinary postal service.

I've chosen to work with Bernadine and Saunders Real Estate. I rent my flat through them and I'm happy with the service.

The most likely buyers are developers who'll want the building but not the business. Should we start running down the stock now? Selling it to other stores when we can?

Please let me know what you think.

Sophia

Henry

I wake on the fiction couch deeply hungover, my head cracking with the light, and Rachel telling me to get up. She's holding my eyelids open like she used to do years ago when we'd stayed up all night talking and then slept through the morning alarm. '*Get. Up.* Henry.'

'What time is it?' I ask, batting off her hands so I can close my eyes again.

'It's eleven. The shop's been open for an hour. There are customers asking for books I can't find. George is yelling at a guy called Martin Gamble who's here to help create the database. And as a separate issue, Amy is waiting in the reading garden for you.'

'Amy's here?' I sit up and mess my hair around. 'How do I look?'

Rachel declines to answer on the grounds that, technically, I'm now her boss, and she doesn't want to start her new job by insulting me.

'Thank you,' I say. 'I appreciate that.'

I pull the blanket around my shoulders, and the customer looking in the classics section gives me a sympathetic look. I give him one back because, as much as I love books, if you're in the classics section first thing in the morning, then there's something not entirely right with your life either.

As I walk toward Amy, who looks fantastic in a blue dress, I'm thinking about the strange dreams I had last night. In the first, Amy was invisible. I knew she was there, but as hard as I tried, I couldn't see her. In the second, I was talking to Rachel in the girls' toilets, and in the last, I was kissing Rachel on the mouth. It was good in the dream, and the memory of it is highly unsettling. God, I hope I didn't kiss her. What if I tried to kiss her? I'll never hear the end of it. The more I think about it, though, the more I think I *did* kiss her. I can feel her lips in a way that doesn't feel like dream lips.

Amy touches my arm as I sit next to her, and we stare at each other for a while. 'You smell like beer,' she says, which is true but not encouraging. I move a little away from her and try to breathe in the opposite direction.

'I'm sorry about last night,' she says eventually. 'I should have told you about Greg, but it happened really quickly. And, I guess, if I'm honest, really honest, I've always been a little bit in love with Greg Smith.'

There should be a disconnect button you can push when someone leaves: you've fucked me over, therefore I no longer love you. I'm not asking for the button to be connected to an ejector seat that removes them from the universe, just one small button that removes them from your heart.

'Are you listening?' Amy asks.

'It all happened very quickly, but if you're honest, you've always been a little bit in love with Greg Smith,' I say.

I should tell her to leave. I should maintain what dignity I can, which isn't much considering she's telling me all this while I'm wearing a blanket and the smell of last night's beer. But my family is pretty shit at dignity as well as love, so I think: fuck dignity. Dignity is not in my genes.

'See, this is why I'm confused,' I tell Amy. 'Because when you told me you loved me, in this bookshop, you didn't say, "I love you, but if I'm honest, I'm also a little bit in love with that moron, Greg Smith." I'd remember that. You just said, "I love you, Henry." And when we bought the plane tickets, and I used *all* my money, you didn't say, "Keep in mind, I'm a little bit in love with Greg Smith."'

'You used all your money *and* some of mine,' she says, and I need her to be honest. I need to know why she's choosing Greg over me.

'Is it because of where I work? How much I earn?' Or, how much I don't earn. 'Is it that I live with my family? Is it because I drove you to the prom in the bookshop van?'

'Henry,' she says, like this is something neither of us needs to get into. But I know her. I know her expressions. I know the one she's wearing now: it's pity. I've seen it on her face when she's watching documentaries about stray animals that no one wants because they're too scruffy. I'm a hundred per cent right about why she chose Greg Smith. He's richer, he's neater, he's going to college.

'Let's not argue. You're a great friend. But we're not in high school anymore.'

'So I'm right.'

'No,' she says, when she clearly means *yes*. She shakes her head, trying to find the answer for me. 'He's the one I always saw myself with. You know, at college. Doing things.'

She puts her hand on my arm for a second, lets me feel the warmth of her. She looks past me into the bookshop, and says, 'There's always Rachel. She still likes you.'

'It's you,' I tell her. 'Not Rachel. *You.*'

She smiles and holds my arm a little tighter.

'What if I changed?' I ask, and she hesitates a little before she answers.

'I don't think it would matter. It wouldn't matter.' It's the first part of her answer that's the truth. She doesn't *think* it would matter, meaning it *might* matter. It *could* matter.

I make her promise that if I change and it does make a difference to her, then she'll come back. She kisses me good-bye and I take it for a yes.

There's not one part of me that doesn't hurt this morning: my teeth, my head, my heart, my pride, my eyeballs. The backs of my eyeballs hurt. I put my head under the water stream and try to wash out the thought of Amy always being a little bit in love with Greg.

I get out of the shower and dry myself off; then I sit on the edge of the bath and let the leftover steam clear my head. Dad walks in as it's clearing, and asks if he can use the mirror.

'Rachel told me about Amy,' he tells me.

'She's only with Greg temporarily.'

'Sometimes you have to let go, Henry,' he says, tapping his

razor on the side of the sink. He doesn't believe that, though. If he did, he'd be moving on with his life instead of rereading *Great Expectations* and hoping for another chance from Mum.

I watch him making roads through the foam on his face, trying to figure out how to say what I want to say, and also trying to figure out if I really want to say it. I'm pretty sure I do.

'How much, Dad?' I ask, and he knows what I'm talking about.

'We own the building, Henry. It's two stories with a big backyard. I'd say well over a million.'

I go quiet, and he finishes off his face, wiping it with the towel I pass him. 'It's ok to want to sell,' he says.

In my perfect world I wouldn't worry about money. In my perfect world books would be with us forever and everyone would love secondhand books as much as Dad and George and I do. Amy would love them. But it's not my perfect world. 'I think maybe we should sell. Mum thinks we should, and she knows about the business.'

He nods, and waits. Because I can't answer with a maybe. It's a yes-or-no question. It reminds me of how he told me once that the thing he loved about fiction was that there were rarely yes-or-no answers when it came to characters. The world is complex, he told me. Humans are too.

He and I have had hundreds of conversations about the characters in books in the store. The last one we had was about *Vernon God Little,* a book by D. B. C. Pierre. I'd loved it enough to read it twice.

'What did you love?' Dad had asked.

'Vernon,' I'd said, naming the main character. 'And the way it's critiquing America. But mainly it's the language. It's like he's left the words out in the sun to buckle a while, and they don't sound like you'd expect.'

'You might like to be a writer one day,' Dad had said. 'What do you think?' Anything, in our bookshop, was possible.

But anything isn't possible. Clearly, it's not, or Mum wouldn't want to sell. She loves the store as much as we all do, and she accepts that the business is dying. Anything will not be possible if, for the rest of my life, I earn the same wage I do now. Anything won't be possible for George.

'Yes,' I say now, running my toe along a crack in the tile. 'I want us to sell.'

'And what will you do?' he asks.

'There's still the possibility of traveling with Amy. I'll probably study next year.'

'Then it's decided,' he says sadly. 'I'll get things under way.'

I walk downstairs and start to detach myself from the bookstore. I don't look at the Letter Library on the way past. I don't check *Prufrock* for strangers' thoughts. I don't look behind me to the reading garden.

I walk straight to the front counter, where George is yelling at the new guy: 'If you don't get your computer out of the way, I'll shove it up your arse.' It's a lawsuit waiting to happen. I take the stapler out of George's hand, because we're a secondhand bookstore and we can't afford to replace an eye.

The new guy – Martin – is about George's age. He seems like a neat, good-looking computer geek.

'Hi,' he says to me, and smiles.

He seems like a *nice*, neat, good-looking computer geek. Or maybe he just seems like a geek next to George in her black clothes and her black hair with a blue stripe running down it. Away from my goth sister, he's probably more popular-guy-in-high-school than geek, which might account for why George doesn't like him.

'I'm Henry,' I say, holding out my hand for him to shake.

'Martin Gamble,' he says, and George says, 'Martin *Charles* Gamble,' in the same way she might say the words *complete and utter dick*.

Martin doesn't look angry: he looks kind of amused. 'Your mum hired me to help in the store and to catalog the books. Which is why,' he says to George, 'I need to charge my computer.'

'Mum doesn't live here anymore,' George says. 'Henry is the manager today, and he's about to fire your arse.'

'Excuse me,' I say to Martin. 'I just need to talk to my sister for one minute.'

I motion for George to follow me out on to the street, but it's clear she's not in the mood to listen. She starts yelling before the door's closed, and I really wish she'd stop because I have a cracker of a headache.

'He goes to my school. He's in my class. He used to date Stacy,' she says. 'They're still friends.'

George doesn't tell me a lot about what school is like for her, but I know about Stacy. She's in the popular crowd and she's not a big fan of anyone who's *not* in the popular crowd, and so not a big fan of my sister's. George told me once that Stacy liked to write GEORGE JONES IS A FREAK on things like toilet doors and lockers and desks.

I peer through the window at Martin. 'He doesn't look like the kind of guy who'd call you a freak. Let's give him a week's trial.'

'No,' she says, and it's clear she's not changing her mind, so I try a different approach.

'Think about how miserable you could make him in a week if you're his boss.'

I can see the idea hadn't occurred to her before, and now that it's been pointed out, it really appeals. She looks through the window at Martin and considers it for a while. 'OK. But he can't bring his friends here. This is my home.'

'Fair enough,' I say, and then I tell her there's something else she needs to know before she goes back inside. I say it quickly. There's no point in dragging it out. 'I voted with Mum. We're definitely selling.'

It's not a huge surprise. She nods and says she figured I would. I can't tell if she thinks it's the right decision. 'If it's not what you want, you should vote against it.'

'No,' she says. 'It's fine. I vote with you.'

I try to imagine George living away from the shop, but I can't. She's basically in one of three places – here, Shanghai Dumplings, or school. And she hates school, so there are only two places that she loves. There are three people that she loves, though: me, Mum, and Dad. She already feels bad because she chose to stay in the bookshop and not move in with Mum. If she votes with Dad, then she's divided the family down the middle. As it is now, I'm the one who's divided the family and she's just going along with me.

We walk back inside, and I soon hear her telling Martin she's his boss and he can't bring his friends in and he has to do what she says.

'OK,' he says, smiling at her in a way that makes her blush, something I've never actually seen before.

. . .

After the morning's emergencies have been dealt with, I turn my attention to Rachel. We've got some catching up to do. Dad's given her the job of cataloging the Letter Library and Martin the job of cataloging the rest of the store.

She's set up a small desk near the Library, with her computer on it, a notebook and a jar of pens. It's typical Rachel. She loves being organized. She loves stationery. She was the kind of girl who always had a never-ending supply of those little fluorescent sticky notes and she wrote on them, word for word, what the teacher said. Then, after she'd written on a note, she'd peel it off and press it to the appropriate page of her novel, like that solved the mystery of that word and why the author had put it on the page. I can still see the neat square of her nail as she did it. I found one of those notes about a month after she'd moved. It had slipped from one of her novels, and it read: *This line sums up the meaning of everything.* Loose from the book, it was tantalizing and completely useless.

'So how was Year 12?' I ask her as a way of starting the conversation.

'OK,' she says without stopping what she's doing, which is alphabetizing the books in the Letter Library.

'So you got into marine biology?' I ask, and she nods and keeps ordering the books.

'And Cal, how's Cal?'

'Henry, I have work to do,' she says. 'Cataloging the Library is a huge job, and your dad wants it done within the month, which, honestly, isn't possible even if I worked day and night.'

'I'll help. We'll do it together.'

'I don't want your help, Henry,' she says in a sharp voice.

'Are we fighting?' I ask. 'It feels like we're fighting.'

'We're not fighting. I need to concentrate, that's all. I'm better off alone.'

I decide to just come right out and ask her: 'Did we kiss last night?'

'Sure, we kissed,' she says. 'And then I went into the bathroom and drank water from the bowl.'

'A simple no would have been fine, Rachel,' I tell her, and walk back to the counter feeling certain that something must have happened last night that I can't remember.

'She found you next to a sanitary disposal unit,' George says helpfully when we talk about it later on Saturday.

Sure, that's embarrassing for me, but that wouldn't make her angry. I serve customers and watch her. Serve and watch. I definitely remember her saying we were friends. Good friends. I remember her apologizing for not writing. So that leaves something in the blank spaces.

Lola walks into the bookshop around one o'clock, and I ask her what she remembers. It's nothing that I don't, just a recap of me falling down and crawling into the girls' toilets.

'You really shouldn't drink,' she says.

'That fact has been more than established.'

'So,' she says, taking a mint from the bowl next to the register. 'The Hollows are breaking up. Hiroko told me last night that she's moving to America to study percussion. So we're over. Done. Four years of working and it's all for nothing.' She throws a mint at my head and it bounces off toward the specials' table. 'Sorry. That made me feel better.'

'Glad to be of help.'

'I just got us another regular gig at Hush. Now I'll have to cancel.'

'You could advertise for a replacement.'

'There's no replacement for Hiroko. There's no other person I can write with. No other person I want to perform with. She's going, so the Hollows are done. We're playing our last gig this Valentine's Day at Laundry. End of story.'

She throws another mint at my head and I move a little so it hits me, because this is bad news and I don't have anything to say that'll cheer her up. The Hollows has been Lola's obsession, her love, pretty much her sole entire focus since she and Hiroko met in the line for Warpaint tickets in Year 8.

I serve some customers and when I come back, Lola's looking across at the Letter Library. 'You're right. Rachel looks mad.' She walks over to do some investigating on my behalf.

They talk. I hear some laughter. Rachel shakes her head and keeps shifting the books into order. Lola watches her and they talk for a while longer.

'You're not fighting,' she says when she comes back. 'You both agreed to be friends last night. You did kiss her, but she's OK about it. You made her miss her ex, Joel, that's all.'

I try to look happy about this because I am happy about it. If I'm not happy about it, then I'm the kind of guy who cares more about his ego than he does about his best friend. And I'm not that guy. 'The kiss must have been good, though. If it made her miss Joel.'

'The quality of the kiss was not discussed,' she says, and writes an address on a piece of paper. 'Justin Kent's having a party this Friday night. Hiroko and I are playing what will be our third-to-last gig. Invite Rachel. She needs cheering up.'

Easier said than done, I think, and go back to my watching.

By Friday I'm deeply, deeply confused.

Every day of the week I've been friendly to her, and every day I've expected Rachel to turn into her old self. Every day she's arrived at work on time, and walked past me, straight over to the Letter Library. She doesn't take a break till lunch, when she disappears for half an hour. She doesn't go to Frank's. I know, because I've gone in to look for her.

Martin's getting the same silent treatment from George. At least, he's getting the silent treatment if he's lucky. If he's not, she's ordering him around and timing his breaks. 'We don't pay enough to time breaks,' I remind her on Wednesday, and she reminds me back that Martin is on trial, and she's his boss, so I should stay out of it.

Strangely, Martin seems to enjoy his interactions with George. There's nothing she can do that he doesn't find funny or weird but, on the whole, likeable.

'What are you reading?' he asks George on Friday afternoon.

'Kafka's *Metamorphosis*,' she says without looking up.

'And what's it about?'

'Guy turns into a giant bug and eventually dies.'

'Not exactly life-affirming,' Martin observes.

'Life isn't exactly life-affirming,' George says.

'How have you been able to read so many books?' he asks,

and she looks up from Kafka, her thumb marking the page. 'I'm a weird girl in high school. I've had some time to kill.'

She stands and Ray Bradbury jumps from her lap to Martin's. He scratches the cat behind the ears and Ray stars purring. 'Traitor,' George says, and I decide that this ends tonight. 'We're going out to Justin Kent's party. All of us. It's a work outing.'

'Am I getting paid?' George asks.

'No.'

'Then I'm not going,' she says, and walks out the front door toward Frank's.

'She'll come,' I tell Martin. I don't tell him it's because Mum stopped by during the week and saw how George was treating him and threatened to dock her pay if she didn't start making him feel welcome.

I've had a lot of conversations with Martin this week, and most of them have had something to do with George. The more I talk to him, the more I like him. He's seen George at her worst, and he likes her. 'She's funny,' he said the other day while I was helping him with the cataloging. 'Funny. Smart. Original.' These are good reasons to like George. These are her best qualities.

What he and George need is some time away from the shop to get to know each other. Rachel and I need that too. Three years have passed, and maybe the problem is we need to connect again. Get to know our new selves.

This is what I tell her this afternoon when I walk over to remind her about the party.

'I have to work tonight,' she says. 'I have to do the hugely insane job your dad has given me,' she says. 'I think he's having a midlife crisis. Not only does he want me to alphabetize all of the books, because people keep putting them back out of order, and not only does he want a record of all of the books in the Library, he also wants a record of anything loose inside the books, like letters, *and* a record of any notations in the margins.'

'That sounds to me like something you'd enjoy,' I tell her.

'A mindlessly boring and pointlessly never-ending task?'

'You love those kinds of tasks. You loved memorizing the periodic table when you were a kid.'

'That wasn't mindlessly boring or pointless. The periodic table lists all the elements existing on the earth. There's a *point* to the periodic table. There's no *point* to this Library. This Library is the definition of pointless, Henry.'

'OK. Enough,' I say. 'More than enough. You've been in a shitty mood all week, and I feel the need to call it to your attention that I am heartbroken and I need some cheering up. I need my best friend back, and I need her to come to a party with me tonight.'

She starts to argue, but I tell her I won't take no for an answer. 'Leave now and be back at the bookshop by nine. You need to drive George because I want you to talk to her about Martin on the way. I want to know what she's thinking.'

'She's thinking she wants you to butt out of her life, Henry.'

She packs up her computer and the rest of her things and leaves without saying that she'll definitely go tonight. I wave at her through the window as she's getting into her car. She waves her middle finger back at me.

'We're all set,' I tell Martin before he leaves. 'I have a great feeling about tonight.'

Pride and Prejudice and Zombies

by Jane Austen and Seth Grahame-Smith

Letters left between pp. 36 and 37
January 15, 2016

Dear George,

I'm looking forward to the party tonight. I think it'll be fun.

Martin

P.S. I like the idea of the Letter Library.

Martin,

Never write to me in this book again.

George

Dear George,

It's lovely to get your reply. You're as charming in print as you are in person. Why can't I write to you in this book? I see you checking it all the time.

                                        Martin

Martin,

I check it because I write to someone else in this book. It's our book. Not your book.

                                        George

Dear George,

Can I write to you in another book? We work together. I'd like to be friends. Please? It's a LONG day, cataloging all the books in the store. I'm typing out the names of EVERY SINGLE BOOK here. No matter what you think I've done (What have I done to you??), it can't be so bad as to make me do this with NO relief.

                                        Martin

Martin,

You hang out with the girl who calls me a freak on a regular basis.

                                        George

Dear George,

I've never called you a freak. I don't think you are a freak. In fact, I've been trying to be your friend at school since you started. You're the one who ignores me and insults me on a regular basis. Do you have any evidence of me being a bad guy?

In the whole time that I've known you, I've done nothing but tell Stacy I think you're an interesting person. It seems to me that you're treating me like Stacy treats you. I think, at the very least, you should give me a trial as your friend, as well as your employee. It's summer. Can't we forget how we are at school? Maybe we could call a truce?

Martin

Martin,

OK. You can write to me, I suppose. But NOT in this book. Write to me in Peter Temple's The Broken Shore. I saw you reading it, and there's a copy in the Letter Library - leave your letters between pages 8 and 9.

George

Dear George,

I'm absolutely overwhelmed by your offer of friendship. Thank you. Really, thank you. It's almost too much. I look forward to all future correspondence.

Martin

Rachel

I leave Howling Books, making sure Henry sees my raised middle finger. I wave it for impact and sound the horn so Martin knows I'm ready. I don't want to drive him home, but on the first day Sophia offered to fill up my car with petrol if I took him because he has to be back by six to look after his sister till his mums finish work. It means he and I have to leave by five, which is a plus for me.

I'm ready to go as soon as I walk in the door each morning and stand in front of the Letter Library and start my job of cataloging the random, boring thoughts of every person who's passed through these pages.

'It's a big job, and it's not what Sophia hired you for, exactly,' Michael said on my first day. 'Martin can do the rest of the shop, but this is what I'd like you to catalog. I want a record of all the books, any letters or things left behind in them, and a record of the main comments.'

'The main comments?' I asked, and looked from the top shelf to the bottom, making an estimate of the number of books – five hundred, at least.

'Yes. The notes in the margins. Words circled or underlined would be good as well, but that might be too much.'

'You think?' I stopped myself before I said he was crazy.

He walked off and left me standing there, feeling like I did at school after the funeral when everything the teachers asked me to do seemed stupid and overwhelming, and all I wanted to do was sleep.

Martin finally gets in the car. He puts on his seat belt without saying a word. I told him on our first trip that I'm a new driver and he shouldn't take it personally but I need to drive in total silence. 'The radio doesn't bother me. Just actual voices in the car.'

I introduced the ban because it's easier than answering his questions about Cal. I've been dodging questions all week about the beach, about Year 12, about Cal, Mum, and college. It turns out even Martin knew Cal because they went to school together.

I wasn't planning on keeping the lie I started at Laundry going, but on her way out of the store on Saturday morning, Amy asked me what college I got into, and there was no way I was telling her I'd failed. George was listening when I told her I was taking a year off, and I haven't been able to walk it back from there.

Even if I wanted to tell Henry, there's been no room in our conversations – he talks constantly about Amy. What's worse than having to catalog pointless love letters that won't ever arrive because they're mailed into the page of a book? Having to listen to Henry talk about his love for Amy while I'm doing it.

. . .

Martin and I cross the river and the world gets greener. I drop him at his house, and on the way back I drive past his and George's school, Cal's old one. The spire on the cathedral makes me want to cry for some reason I can't work out.

Sometimes I let myself cry when I'm alone, but not today because I'm on the way to see Gus. Rose was the one who originally suggested Gus as a therapist. They're old friends from medical school, and she knew he lived near Sea Ridge. He called the warehouse on Monday to see how I was settling in and to let me know he'd be in the city this afternoon. If I felt like talking, I should meet him at St. Albert's. 'Call into the ER and get Rose to page me.'

The ER is only a short walk away from the parking lot. I'm inside before I've thought through how much it'll remind me of when Mum, Gran and I waited for the news. Two hours of praying that Cal was alive, certain the whole time that he wasn't.

There are three people waiting on the chairs in the corner. They're holding hands, all three of them, a pile of knuckles resting in the lap of the person in the middle. She looks like the grandmother. The girl on the left, with her desperate eyes, reminds me of me. The third woman looks like a mother. I make the mistake of looking directly into the girl's eyes.

I walk out of the waiting room and into the air. I'm planning on getting into my car and driving away when I see Gus walking toward me. He's got two coffees stacked in one hand, and he's waving at me with the other.

He looks behind me at the EMERGENCY sign and frowns. We walk across the road to the park and sit on a bench under a huge old maple to drink our coffees.

'Sorry about the meeting place,' he says, and I tell him it's fine.

'It doesn't seem fine,' he says.

'There were people in there who look like us. Like me and Mum and Gran.'

'And how do you look?' he asks.

'Sad,' I snap at him, and he takes a drink from his coffee and tells me I don't seem sad today. 'You seem kind of angry.'

'Intuitive,' I say, and he tells me to stop being a smart aleck and tell him what's wrong.

'Where does that phrase *smart aleck* come from?' I ask, buying myself some time. 'Henry would probably know. His dad would definitely know.'

'Do you like working with them?' Gus asks.

'Michael, Henry's dad, has me cataloging the Letter Library.' I explain what it is and how frustrating I'm finding the job.

'Does it pay you enough?' Gus asks, and I nod. 'And it's a nice place to work?'

'I can set my own hours. I get breaks whenever I need them, I don't have to serve customers unless Henry or George are on a break. Martin's nice, the guy who's been hired to catalog the rest of the store.'

'If it's just the monotony that's getting to you, wear headphones. Listen to music.'

'That'd stop the questions, I guess. People are asking about Cal.' I watch a blue wren moving near our feet. I let myself get mesmerized by the detail of it. 'I haven't told them he's dead.'

'Maybe that's what's bothering you?' Gus asks.

'It's that I don't have patience for pointless stuff anymore. I mean, what's Michael planning on doing with my catalog? It'll sit in a file on his computer, and one day he'll delete it and I'll have done all that work for nothing. Seems stupid when there are more important things to do.'

'What more important things have you got to do?' Gus asks. 'I'm just curious.'

When I don't answer, he tells me to try writing about what's making me angry.

I really like Gus. More than that, I respect him. But today I want to tell him to fuck off so badly I have to cover my mouth with my hands so the two words don't escape.

We spend the rest of our time staring at the blue wren, picking at food we can't see, somewhere under the grass.

I pull up at the bookstore at nine, and see George waiting outside the door. As soon as she sees my car, she calls out she's leaving to Henry and gets in the front seat. 'Let's go,' she says. 'If we get to the party before them, we can lose ourselves in the crowd.'

It's not a bad idea, so I start the engine and let George direct me to Justin's house. I remember Justin from high school. He was a nice guy, a little wild, but OK. His parents always seemed to be away, so his house was available for parties. The last night of the world party was at his house, I think. I'm wondering who I might see – Amy, for certain – when George nudges me out of my thoughts and tells me to take a left at the light.

She turns on the radio and skips around until she finds a station playing David Bowie, and then leans back and says, 'So how's Cal?'

I can't dodge questions for much longer and not in a small

space like this, so I wind down the window and tell her he's good. I just leave out the part where he's ash in an urn on my mum's mantelpiece. I'm surprised George even remembers Cal. I knew they went to the same school, but I can't imagine their paths crossed that often.

Cal was a tall, skinny guy with a cloud of brown hair that made him look kind of like a dandelion. A dandelion with glasses, giant headphones around his neck, and a book in his hand. George has long straight black hair with a blue stripe down the left side. These days she has a tattoo running along her collarbone; it's the number *44* written in a soft blue-sky script. I heard Martin asking about the tattoo during the week. 'Forty-four. Is that the meaning of life?' he asked. 'No, that would be forty-two,' she'd said, which is something I know because Cal read *The Hitchhiker's Guide to the Galaxy.*

'But what's he doing?' she asks, and it feels like I'm un-writing him by not filling her in, so I tell her what he would be doing, if he were alive. 'He's on exchange. It's not an official program. He's living with Dad at the moment.'

It's a sort of truth. The plan had been for Dad to spend three months in France so Cal could stay with him. If Cal hadn't drowned, that's where he'd be right now.

'That makes sense,' George says, in a way that makes me think maybe she knew him better than I thought.

'I didn't know him that well,' she says when I ask. 'He was nice to me at school once. He gave me some Sea-Monkeys. He said they're like time travelers. They can hibernate till conditions are better. I haven't put them in water yet. I'm saving them.'

I didn't know that Cal had a crush on George, but he must have. He must have really liked her because he wouldn't have given Sea-Monkeys to just any girl. I look over at her – boots on the dash, humming to Bowie. Then I imagine Cal at school, holding the Sea-Monkeys, trying to get up the courage to give them to George. He probably wrote out a speech beforehand. He'd have worked out exactly when she'd be alone so he could talk to her. I wish he could have lived long enough to have had someone like George fall in love with him. I wish so hard, the car jerks a little.

'Did you talk much?' I ask. 'After that?'

'Not much.'

Cal and I didn't tell each other everything, but I thought I knew most things about him. I thought I knew the important things, and having a crush on a girl feels like one of those. I could be sad about this but it's been such a quiet year, sitting on the beach with only Woof or Mum for company.

So I tell George to turn up the music. There's a Bowie special on, and the next song is 'Young American', which was one of Cal's favorites and is one of George's too. When the chorus comes on, I start singing out the words like Cal would if he were here. It surprises George for a second, and I think she says something about me being as weird as my brother, and then she starts singing too.

Pride and Prejudice and Zombies

by Jane Austen and Seth Grahame-Smith

Letters left between pp. 44 and 45
March 15–April 15, 2014

Dear George,

So how's Year 9 going? I've found this old typewriter that belonged to my grandpa in the shed, so I'm using it for our letters.

The y jumps a little yyyyyyy, see?

I like Year 9. I'm reading a heap – swimming too, but obviously not the two together. I got a new haircut – my sister says I look good. I think I still look weird. My ears are quite big. I've never noticed that before. You have nice ears – they're so small I wonder how you fit all the piercings on them. I'd like to count them one day. Too much information?

Pytheas

Dear Pytheas,

You'd be welcome to count them, if you ever told me who you are?!? You have a new haircut and you have big ears, so I guess there are two clues. No one at school fits that description.

I've been reading a heap too – not swimming. I don't swim. I like baths, though, and they allow the added bonus of being able to read and bathe at the same time.

I just read Fahrenheit 451 *by Ray Bradbury (we have a cat named after him). It's about firemen who burn books. It's made me think about a world where there are no books, and that world worries me. I'm glad I live in a bookstore so we'll never have to be without them. My family would be dying with the books, I'm pretty sure. Henry would go up in flames before he let his collection burn.*

How is Year 9? It's OK, except suddenly Martin Gamble is everywhere I go, laughing at me, flipping up the cover of my book to see what I'm reading. You're not Martin Gamble, are you? I don't think you are, but the thought keeps crossing my mind. He's going out with Stacy, so it's highly unlikely you are. Unless these letters are a joke, which I know they're not. So I've just convinced myself that you're not Martin.

On another, sadder note, my parents are fighting a lot. They fight quietly and it scares me. Dad says they won't ever divorce, not as long as their copy of Great Expectations is in the Letter Library. It's their book. Dad says it reminds them of how much they love each other, but I don't know. They don't seem to love each other at the moment, and I don't want to point it out but Pip and Estella don't even end up together.

Bye for now,
George

Dear George,

I was really upset when my parents divorced. I still miss Dad, and I'm planning on spending some time with him overseas soon. But it gets easier. Or, you get used to it being hard.

No, I'm not Martin Gamble. He's actually pretty nice. Maybe he's trying to talk to you?

Pytheas

Henry

George leaves as soon as Rachel arrives, telling me she's very keen to get away from Martin. I'm not fooled. I asked her to give me a makeover this evening, because I'm almost certain Amy will be at the party tonight, and while she did my hair I said I was pretty sure that Martin liked her. She didn't tell me to shut up.

I say this to Martin on the way to the party and quiz him about how he feels.

'Are you always like this?' he asks.

'Like what?'

'Like a matchmaker.'

'I would prefer my sister to be happy,' I tell him. 'I think it's possible you could restore her faith in life and love.'

'No pressure there,' he says.

'Do you like her?' I ask.

'I do,' he admits. 'I've liked her for a while. It was part of the reason I took the job at the bookstore. One of my mums had some clerical work for me at her office, but then I saw this cataloging job advertised at Howling Books, so I took it.'

'Try to kiss her tonight,' I say.

'I don't think that will work. George seems like a slow mover, so I think I'll take my time. I've been writing to her this week.'

'Nice move,' I say. 'She'll like that.'

'She doesn't seem to entirely like it, but she doesn't seem to dislike it as much as she did.'

We pull up at the party, and I see Amy walking in. 'Do I look OK?' I ask Martin, and he says he thinks so. 'George did a good job.'

'But do I look responsible?'

He scratches his neck and thinks about it. 'I guess. You are responsible. You run a bookstore.'

'I run a secondhand bookstore that doesn't earn very much,' I tell him, drawing an important distinction before I get out of the car.

The first person I see when I walk inside is Rachel. I can tell by the way she looks at me that George really did do a good job. 'I'm pleasing to the eye, aren't I?' I ask.

'Hard to tell,' she says. 'I'm blinded by your ego.'

'Hilarious,' I say, watching Martin disappearing down the corridor. 'He told me in the car that he likes her.'

'He told you or you badgered it out of him?'

'He offered the information after some persuasive questioning.'

'George seemed very keen to get here early so she could avoid him. Stop trying to set her up.'

'Are you planning on fighting with me all night?'

'Only if you keep saying stupid things,' she says as we walk into the living room, which is full of people who are really dressed up. 'You didn't mention it was an eighteenth birthday,' she says, looking at the balloons. 'Or that it would be formal.'

'It's not really formal,' I say as a girl in pink walks past.

Rachel waves at the air in front of her. 'I'm choking on taffeta and perfume, Henry.'

'Lola didn't mention it was this kind of party. But you look good in old jeans,' I say, and she walks toward the kitchen to get some water. Amy and Greg are in there, both of them looking like they peeled themselves off the pages of a magazine. He's in a suit – a very cool suit, I have to admit. She's in a gold dress that actually stops me breathing for a second.

Like Rachel, I'm not in formal wear. If news isn't music-related, Lola frequently forgets to pass it on. I grab two waters and lead Rachel out into the backyard so we can hide from all the formally attired people.

The Hollows are setting up on what looks like a rented stage. We sit in the front row and give Lola a wave. We watch her intently so we don't have to talk, but after around five minutes Lola does her test of the microphone: 'Testing, you two are freaking me the fuck out, stop staring and talk to each other, testing.'

'So did I do anything else stupid last Friday night, apart from what I've already heard?' I ask, trying to make some conversation.

'Many, many things,' Rachel answers.

'Like?'

'You sang,' she says.

'Troubling. What song?'

'"I Will Always Love You" by Whitney Houston.'

'More troubling. Anything worse than that?'

'Is there anything worse than that?' she asks.

'I could have been wearing white leather during the rendition.'

'No leather. Just some dramatic hand gestures.' She does a small reenactment of me dancing that's disturbingly accurate.

I can't stop picking out the differences in her. I've been doing it all week. I used to know everything – down to the scar she had on the back of her knee, a downward-running river from where she backed up on to a sharp stick in a fence in Year 7. Now it feels like we're getting to know each other again. 'It's strange, isn't it? Seeing each other again.'

'I guess,' she says.

'Give me a break, Rachel. I'm trying, here. Fill me in.'

'Fill you in?'

'Boys. School. Friends. You've been avoiding questions all week.'

'There's nothing much to tell,' she says.

She moves her chair back a little so some people can pass, and because I'm still staring at her and I haven't dropped the subject, she says, 'OK. Well, you know about the guy – Joel Winter.'

'Your ex.'

'Sort of. Yes. I don't know. We left things undecided.'

'Do you have a picture?' I ask as the Hollows start playing.

She shakes her head.

'Not on your phone?'

She gives in and takes out her phone and shows me. 'He looks like Greg Smith,' I say, and she puts the phone back into her pocket. 'I didn't mean to insult him. I meant he's good-looking.'

'OK, you have to stop being pathetic,' she says. 'You have to stop thinking about her, staring at her, wanting her. Just stop. And if you can't actually do it, then you have to at least pretend that you're forgetting her because she won't come back if you're chasing her. That's not Amy's style.'

I am being pathetic, she's correct. But surely right now I'm allowed to be pathetic and my friends just have to deal with it and not point it out. 'This is the time you tell me how great I am.'

She doesn't say anything. Rachel's come back as an entirely different person. She's rude. She's been rude all week, and not just to me. She's been rude to my dad too.

There's a break in the music, and I use it to tell Rachel exactly what I think. 'You've changed, and not in a good way. You used to be fantastic. You used to be funny and interesting. You always had people's backs. But now you're rude – to me, to my dad, which is shitty. You're rude to George and Martin.'

'I've been driving him home,' she points out.

'Because my mum pays for your petrol and it means you can leave at five. You won't even let him speak in the car.' I take a breath. 'You haven't been here for three years. You haven't written, you clearly don't give a shit about me, and now you come back calling me pathetic. And you're complaining about cataloging the Letter Library, telling me my dad's having a midlife crisis – which he might well be, but maybe that's understandable given that he's losing the bookshop. Meanwhile, I've lost Amy, and George is missing Mum. What have you lost, Rachel? Apart from your sense of humor?'

She raises her middle finger at me.

'Very grown-up,' I say, and she raises her other one.

'If you don't want to work at the bookshop, don't. If you don't want to be at the party, leave. You have a car.'

'Thanks for reminding me, Henry,' she says, and then she tips the last of her water down the front of my jeans and walks out.

. . .

I sit here shifting between feeling terrible about what I said to Rachel and feeling good because I stood up for myself and most of all feeling like I've wet myself because of Rachel's parting move.

After about half an hour, Martin walks over and sits next to me. 'Great party,' he says, like what he's really saying is, *This is the shittest place I have ever been in my whole life. Fuck you for bringing me here.* Even when he's being rude, Martin is polite.

'You seemed to be saying in the car that I should make a move on George,' he continues. 'That if I made a move on her, she would welcome that move.'

'I thought you weren't planning on making the move.'

'I wasn't. And then I changed my mind because we'd been talking to each other for an hour and I was making her laugh, and she was leaning close to me and it seemed like you were right and it'd be OK to kiss her.'

'But I was wrong?'

'You were wrong,' he says. 'She did not welcome a move. I am definitely not attractive to her and she's in love with someone else.'

This is news to me. 'Who?'

'I don't know. Someone who is attractive to her, presumably.' He shakes his head a little, like he can't make sense of the evening in any way. '"You think you're so hot," she said. I don't think I'm hot. I think I'm geeky. I think I'm a geeky guy who likes computers and wants to be a lawyer.'

While he's talking a text comes in from George, saying she's going home with Rachel. I give Lola and Hiroko a wave good-bye, and I tell Martin that I'll drive him home. 'It's possible the party wasn't a great idea,' I say as we walk to the front lawn, where Greg is standing with Amy. 'They just keep turning up around me. He's doing it deliberately.'

'I like Rachel better than Amy,' Martin says, as if it's even relevant.

'She doesn't let you speak in the car,' I remind him.

'She lets me choose the radio station. She lets me eat in the car. She stops if I need to buy something on the way home. She just doesn't talk.'

Before I can answer, Greg points at my jeans and calls out: 'Couldn't find the bathroom?'

'Don't be an idiot, Greg,' Amy says, which gives me some small hope that she will realize, in time, that he can't *not* be an idiot, because that's how he's made.

'I'm not the one who wet myself,' he says.

I should be mature and walk away from Greg. But I'm not mature, as evidenced by my life. I pick up the garden hose that's sitting by my feet. It's got a pressure nozzle, which is convenient. I don't hose Greg all over. I get him where Rachel got me. Exactly there. It gives me great satisfaction that I probably ruined a very expensive suit.

While Greg is yelling at us, Martin and I walk to the van, get in, and I drive us away.

Rachel

What have I lost? What have I *lost*? Only everything, you complete moron. I've lost more than you, that's for absolutely sure. I've lost Cal; I've lost the old Mum, the old me. I've lost an *entire ocean*. That's 71 per cent of the earth, that's 99 per cent of the biosphere. I've lost 99 per cent of the biosphere, and you've lost Amy.

You've lost a girl who, the last time I checked, dotted her *i*'s with tiny little self-portraits. A girl who checks her reflection in the mirror every other minute of the day. A girl who watches you fall on the floor in front of her and doesn't help you up.

I'm throwing myself through the crowd, my mind on the car, on my getaway, on maybe driving off and leaving this city behind to go to another city, away from the job and Henry and Rose, when George touches the edge of my T-shirt and asks me for a lift home.

I pretend not to notice that she's crying. I tell her Henry's in the backyard and that she should go find him. I'm not going home. I don't know where I'm going, exactly, but it's not back to the bookstore or back to the warehouse. She walks away from me, through the crowd, and past a group of girls who laugh at her. George stops and says something to them but she's outnumbered and she's already crying, so all they do is laugh more.

I recognize one of the girls. Cal and Tim pointed Stacy out in the yearbook once. 'She basically runs the place,' Cal said. 'If she doesn't like you, then no one likes you.'

'Does she like you?' I asked them, and Tim answered that they were in the fortunate position of Stacy not knowing they were alive.

George isn't in that fortunate position tonight. Cal would hate me for not helping her. I have the strange, impossible feeling that he's actually here, watching me.

I walk over and pull George away from the girls. Her hand feels small and warm. It holds me back like it needs to be held, so I don't let it go. I hold it all the way across the lawn, past Amy and Greg, past people sitting on the fence. I hold it till we reach the car.

Before she gets in, she texts Henry to let him know she's with me, and then silently puts away her phone. She still hasn't said anything by the time we're at the end of the street. 'Are you OK?' I ask, and she puts her face down toward her knees. 'Fuuuuucccck,' she says, and I pull the car over so I can concentrate on her.

'I was talking to Martin,' she says. 'We were hiding in the top-floor bathroom to get away from the crowd. God, Henry's an idiot. He didn't even check if it was formal. So Martin's there with me, his knees leaning against my knees talking about funny things to make me laugh. We're talking for ages and it's great. I don't talk like that with anyone, at least not face to face. And then he leans in and kisses me. It took me by surprise so I pushed him back and it got weird and he said he thought that's what I wanted and I was embarrassed so I told him he needs to get over himself because he thinks he's hot, which he doesn't, and then he walked out before I could fix things and now he feels like an idiot when I'm the idiot.'

'Why are you an idiot?'

'Because I did sort of want to kiss him, but at the same time I like someone else.' She looks at me with mascara-smudged eyes. 'But the "someone else" isn't really an option. I mean, I want him to be an option, but I don't know that he is.'

George is a lot like Henry when she starts talking about something. It's not entirely easy to follow her line of thought.

'The someone else writes to me in the Letter Library. He leaves – at least he was leaving – letters between pages 44 and 45 of *Pride and Prejudice and Zombies*.' She pulls her shirt open a little so I can see the sky-blue *44*.

'Do you know who he is?' I ask, thinking this guy could be anyone.

'I think I do. I'm pretty sure. He hasn't come to get the letters that I've left in the book for a while. I've stopped leaving them.'

'You're certain Martin didn't write them?' I ask, and she says she's sure he didn't.

'I like Martin,' I say, which is all the advice I have. 'He really seems to like you, and he's here and this letter guy isn't.'

'I know,' she says, but it's clear how she feels about him, whether he's good for her or not.

'He's so beautiful,' she says about the letter guy. 'If he's who I think he is, he's the loveliest person I've ever met. And I lie in bed thinking about him, you know?' she asks, and I know, even though I haven't felt that in a long while, I know. 'What should I do?' she asks, and it occurs to me that George can't have that many female friends if she's asking me this question. 'If it were you . . . ,' she says.

I think back to that night when I was desperate for Henry. When Lola and I were laughing and breaking into the bookstore so I could tell him. In hindsight it wasn't my best idea.

'I'd play it safe. I'd wait and see.'

She doesn't know that I wrote Henry the letter, so I just tell her that I loved someone once who didn't love me back. Then I met a boy called Joel, who did. I tell her how good it is when someone you like definitely likes you back without any confusion.

'Did you sleep with Joel?' she asks, and again it occurs to me that George and I are alike. We've both had great brothers but no sisters to ask things. George seems young tonight. She hovers on the edge of the car seat, waiting to hear my answer.

'I did,' I say. 'After a while, and when I was sure. It's a big deal. People might tell you it's not, but it is.'

She asks me about it, and I tell her. And as I do, I almost feel how I did that first night Joel and I were together in his room. His parents were away. We'd already decided. His hands moved over my skin in velvet jolts. The actual act was OK the first time, but it got better the closer we got. The parts that I miss came after, when we lay together in our warmth, talking about the future.

'Be sure,' I tell George, and then I start up the car and take her home.

· · ·

My plan is to deliver George to the bookstore and keep driving. But when we arrive, I look through the window and see Michael talking to Frederick and Frieda over coffee.

It reminds me of nights in Year 9 when they all helped Henry and me with English. The bookstore was always a hub of people who loved books and wanted to talk about them. Michael charged other students for tutoring, but he said I was like a daughter and refused to take my money.

Henry's right. I don't have a sense of humor anymore. I lost my friends in Sea Ridge because of it. They tried to hang in there with me, but I pushed them away, the same way I pushed Joel.

'Are you OK?' George asks.

'Not really,' I say, and follow her inside to talk to Michael.

I ask if I can speak to him alone for a minute, and we walk toward the Letter Library. He puts his hand on the books, the way a person might do to feel the heat from something. 'There's twenty years of history here,' he says, his eyes roaming along the shelves.

I already knew all of the things that Henry reminded me of earlier. I knew that Sophia and Michael had divorced, that they were all losing the bookstore. But my skin's kind of thick since Cal died. All the sadness of losing him is sealed in and no one else's sadness seems to get through.

'I'm sorry I've been rude all week,' I tell Michael, and he accepts my apology without question.

He admits it's a difficult job. 'That's why I chose you.'

'I've finished the alphabetizing, but it took almost the whole week.' I try to strike the right tone – gentle, kind – but I've lost those octaves and my words sound harsh. 'Next week I'll keep inputting the notes. But I think it'll take longer than six months, even with overtime.'

'The job's too big,' he says, with all the octaves that I've lost.

It is, but that's not what I'm trying to tell him. 'If you give me a key to the bookstore, I could work double time. I could catalog when it's quiet and I don't get interrupted by customers.'

'Thank you,' he says, and runs his eyes over the spines of the books. 'You see it's really a library of people,' he explains, and gives me a spare key.

George and her dad go upstairs, and Frederick and Frieda go home. I stay and continue work on the Letter Library, trying to see it as a library of people. If it is, it's people who Michael doesn't know. It's like the box of Cal's belongings in the car. It's leftover stuff that doesn't add up to anything that matters.

I've promised, though. The Letter Library is the heart of the bookstore, and the bookstore is Michael's life. It's Henry's too. I don't know how he's planning on living without it. I keep imagining the whole family returning to the shop the same way Mum and I drifted in and out of Cal's room.

I've been going for an hour, entering people's thoughts and notes into my database, when I pull out the copy of T. S. Eliot's *Prufrock and Other Observations.* I turn to page 22, but of course my love letter's not there. I pull out some books and look behind them. I flick through the books around Eliot, but I don't find anything. A lot of people visit the Library. It's possible some stranger took it before Henry opened the book to read his favorite poem: 'The Love Song of J. Alfred Prufrock.'

He read it to me once, on a night in Year 8 when I stayed

over. We were lying on the floor of the bookshop, and I told him I didn't like poetry. 'I can't understand it, so it never makes me feel anything.'

'Hang on,' he said, and came back with this book from the Letter Library.

He read it to me, and it did feel like a love song. I can hear his voice – *we have lingered in the chambers of the sea.*

I remember that, as he read it, I was staring at a mark on the ceiling – it looked like a tear-shaped sun.

Do I dare disturb the universe? he read, and I don't know what the poem was actually about, but lying there next to him, with his voice so close to my ear, I wanted to disturb something – I wanted to disturb us, shake us out of him seeing me as Rachel, his best friend.

I loved it for those lines that said something to me about life that I couldn't quite understand.

'Explain it to me,' I said.

'I could. But do you need to understand it to love it? You think it's beautiful – that's enough,' he said, and closed the book. 'Proof that you don't hate all poetry.'

He closed his eyes and after a while he started snoring, and I took the book from his sleeping fingers and read the poem again.

Tonight I see the words and phrases that Henry has underlined over the years. I see also that other people have done the same, marking their loved ideas. Back in Year 8, I didn't notice those markings. I didn't notice the title page, either, but tonight I read the inscription:

Dear E, I have left this book in the library, because I cannot bear to keep it, and I cannot throw it away. F.

I know, without any real proof, that E is dead. And that some of the lines in the love song belong to her – that she has been on this page, the same page as Henry and me – and loved the same words that we have loved.

I stop being angry with Henry in the quiet shop. I sit on the floor and read over the poem. I hear it in Henry's voice. I think strange things as I read. How this copy of the book holds the memory of that night with Henry – and it holds the memories of E and F and countless other people, I suppose.

The memories are in the words. And from that the strange thought comes that my memories are trapped in all the copies of this poem, and so everyone who's reading it, no matter what copy, has my memories without knowing it.

I decide to wait for Henry to come home. I take the copy of *Cloud Atlas* out of the window display, put the five dollars for it on the counter, take it over to the fiction couch, and start to read.

Cloud Atlas

by David Mitchell

Note found on title page

> *Dear Grace, on your first day of college. All men (and women) have the desire to know. - Aristotle (and Dad) xxx Enjoy the journey. It's wild and a little confusing, but good, I hope.*

Henry

I take Martin home and we laugh for a while about Greg, and then we both settle into quiet. I'm guessing he's thinking about George. I think about the argument I had with Rachel, which leads to thoughts about her in general, which leads me to the greater mystery of what happened to her and why she's come back angry with me and the whole world.

'She used to be really something,' I say to Martin. 'She killed everyone in races at the school swimming carnival. She won the science prize every year and the math prize, until Amy arrived. Ask her anything about science and she knows the answer. She wants to study fish that live in the deep sea, the scary-arsed ones that dwell in complete darkness.'

'I worry about shark attacks,' Martin says.

'I know, right? But she's not afraid.'

When we're close, Martin directs me to his house, which is

over the river on an avenue lined with trees. It has clapboard siding with a huge fig tree in the front yard. Beyond the tree, I can see two women sitting on the veranda. 'My mums,' he says, and I give them a wave as he gets out of the car.

This side of town reminds me of Amy, because of the way she talked about it. She's never really gotten used to living in Gracetown, and I can see why. I love it, but the streets where I live aren't green like they are over here.

I think about her all the way across the bridge. I think about the potential hopefulness of her realizing that Greg is an idiot, and the way she touched my arm before she left the bookshop. I think about how, so far, she's always come back to me in the end. And so on the way home, I make a detour via her street.

I don't sit on the steps of her apartment building and wait for her; I leave a note in her mailbox:

> *I just don't think he's good enough for you, that's all.*
> *Henry*

Rachel's there when I open the door of the shop. She's reading *Cloud Atlas*, squinting at the pages in the dimness.

'I thought you didn't read fiction,' I say, turning on the light so she can see.

'Maybe I'm changing my ways.'

Cloud Atlas is a set of stories from different times, and Rachel asks me if they're interconnected. 'How does it all fit together?' she asks. This is what Rachel does with fiction – she reads the last page first; she asks me for spoilers. She googles to find out the meaning. 'Is it a novel or a set of short stories? Just tell me that much.'

'No,' I tell her, and she frowns a little and marks her page with a slip of paper.

'Walk with me?' she asks, and I head out with her into the night.

We take the route we took when we were in Year 9 and it was hot and we couldn't sleep. Down High Street, walking a huge block back up to the bookstore. Around again if we felt like it, which was almost every time.

'I'm sorry,' she says. 'About the party. And the things I said about your dad. I apologized to him and said I'd try to finish cataloging.' She smiles. 'Sorry for the drink.'

I tell her about Greg and the hose and she laughs. 'I should have stuck around. You know he used to dislocate body parts to impress girls. He told me in Year 9 that he could dislocate his penis.'

'There's no bone in there. Is there a bone in there?'

'The adult body has two hundred and six bones, and not one of them is there, Henry,' she says.

'So what's he dislocating?'

'This is a mystery I do not need solved,' she says, and hits the button as we stop at the lights.

'I haven't been myself lately,' she says, balancing back on her heels. 'Cal died ten months ago. He drowned.' Then the lights change, and we cross the road.

. . .

I have this stupid thought that it should be raining when she tells me. It should be a different kind of night. It should be starless. It should be bleak. It's the most terrible news I've ever heard, and I can't quite make myself believe it.

I think about the last time I saw him. He came in looking for books on the ocean. I remember he bought a book that I'd found in a thrift shop – *The Log from the Sea of Cortez* by John Steinbeck. I hadn't read it. I'd bought it for the shop because I'd liked *Of Mice and Men* and *The Grapes of Wrath*.

Cal told me the book was about an expedition to the Gulf of California that Steinbeck had made with his closest friend, Ed Ricketts.

They went to collect and observe marine life on the coast, and although I never got around to reading the book, and I've forgotten most of what Cal told me, I haven't forgotten the part about the friendship between a writer and a scientist. It felt right, the balance between those two things. I don't know much about Steinbeck or Ricketts, but I could imagine a scientist and a poet collecting specimens, drawing them, observing them from two different poles of life. I imagined one sparking the thoughts of the other.

I imagined them sitting on the boat at dusk, sunburned, going over their thoughts from the day. Talking late into the night, and really understanding something about the world with the help of science and literature. Like maybe they were half of each other and they were always destined to be friends.

It seems stupid to tell Rachel about one small conversation between Cal and me, when she had millions of them that really meant something, but I tell her anyway, because what else is there?

Rachel swallows and wipes at her eyes and says, 'Thank you,' like somehow it helped, which I can't imagine it did.

I've read about death, obviously, but I've never known anyone who's died. I feel like an idiot now for complaining about Amy breaking my heart. If I lost George, nothing would matter; I can't imagine not having her. I don't know how to imagine it.

Rachel's crying more now, and looking embarrassed. 'I'm not depressed,' she says, like it's the worst thing in the world. And then she says, 'No, I take it back. I am. I'm so depressed, Henry. I'm so depressed my friends at the beach started avoiding me. I broke up with Joel; I couldn't *feel* anything anymore. I see a therapist. I saw him today. God, Henry, I failed Year 12. Everything's a mess.'

I offer her my sleeve so she can wipe her eyes and nose, but she's already using her own. She laughs, and sniffs and blinks and tries to mop up the mascara. 'Did I get it all?'

'Sort of,' I say. 'You look fine. You look good. Anyway,' I continue, 'for the record, I think you should be depressed. I think depression is completely fair enough. Depression is the absolute appropriate response here.'

'It's been nearly a year,' she says, but that doesn't seem like a very long time to me. If George died, I think I'd miss her forever.

'Why didn't you call me? I would have come. I would have come to the funeral.'

She shakes her head, as though she doesn't quite understand it herself.

We decide to go around the block again, and while we're walking Rachel talks. She tells me how her mum just collapsed on the inside after the funeral and hasn't been herself since. She tells me that she collapsed too. How Christmas was this awful meal where they cooked Cal's favorite food but no one ate anything. How there's a box of Cal's things locked in her car trunk.

A summer storm starts. She looks up and then over at me. 'I haven't told anyone here in Gracetown. Please don't tell anyone either. I came back to forget about it for a while.'

I wonder how she could forget about it, a thing like that. And I wonder how she can go on living if she doesn't.

Rachel

It's a relief to tell Henry, to let everything out – losing Cal, how I failed, how everything feels ruined now. It's a relief to cry and have Henry tell me this is the correct response and to hold out his sleeve.

I feel exhausted afterward. I feel almost as tired as I did in those days after we dragged Cal out of the ocean and tried to force him back to life on the beach.

I sit on a bench and I tell Henry I'm not sure I can get up. Sometimes I feel like running, and sometimes I wish I could swim, and sometimes I just want to sit in the same place forever, because I don't have the energy for another day without Cal in it.

The story he told me about *The Log from the Sea of Cortez* is perfect. I can see Cal at the counter of the bookstore, taking mints from the free bowl and rolling them up and down the counter while he spoke to Henry. Cal loved Henry. He loved telling him strange scientific facts when Henry came to our place for Sunday-night pizzas.

After a while it starts to rain softly. There are sparks in the humid sky. 'We need to go,' Henry says. He's not a fan of thunderstorms.

'Maybe I'll just sit here,' I say. 'It'll stop raining soon.'

'No,' he says, and kneels down with his back to me so I can climb on.

He stands and I wrap my legs around his waist and tuck my chin into his neck, like I did as a kid when we were running races in primary school.

'This is much better,' I say as we start walking.

'I'm sure it is,' he says. 'If you're the one on the back.'

'I did save you the other night,' I say. 'So it's payback.'

It really starts raining. 'I forget. Do you stand under a pole in a lightning storm?' Henry asks, moving faster up High Street.

'Sure, and it helps if you can find a puddle too,' I tell him.

'We don't stand under a pole,' he says.

'We don't stand under a pole,' I confirm.

He starts running and it feels good to be weightless and moving and laughing. I count the seconds between the lightning and thunder and tell Henry the charge is at least six kilometers away from us. 'It's not that I don't believe you,' he says, sprinting the last stretch to the bookstore. 'I just don't want to take any chances.'

He stops, fumbles with his keys, and unlocks the door. While he goes upstairs to find us some towels, I text Rose to let her know I'm at the bookstore and I'll probably stay the night.

I don't want to go home. I want to lie on the floor on the quilt bed that Henry used to make when we were kids, and talk and fall asleep.

I say this to Henry when he comes downstairs, and he looks relieved that there's something practical he can do. He makes a three-quilt bed – three on the floor and one to pull over us. Because it's a warm night, we don't really need a top quilt, so we lie on the four, and it's as comfortable as a mattress.

We lie quietly for a while, listening to the creak of the store – someone's footsteps across the ceiling, walking to the bathroom and back in the flat above.

I look out at the rain that's falling beyond the window, lit up by the streetlights so every separate line of water is visible.

'I had a dream where Cal told me he could see the world from above,' I tell Henry. 'He said the seconds were pouring off people, tiny glowing dots pouring from their skins, only no one could see them.'

'Beautiful dream,' Henry says.

'Is it? Wouldn't it be better if the seconds were adding up? Do we have a set amount of seconds to live when we're born or an unknowable number?'

'An unknowable number,' Henry decides.

'How do you know?'

'I don't. I believe.' He rolls over and looks at me. 'I believe I am adding up to something.'

'I don't want to cry anymore,' I tell him. 'I'll think I'm at the end, but then I realize there's more to go. Tonight there was more to go.'

'Have you gone to the top of that cliff in Sea Ridge and just screamed your lungs out?' he asks.

'Done it.'

'Did you swim till you're exhausted?' he asks.

I look right at him because I don't care if he sees how sad I am, that I'm cooked right through with it. 'I hate the water now.' I tell him I can look at it, but I can't stand the thought of diving under. 'It took him,' I say. 'It took him, Henry. The thing I loved took him.'

He stretches out an arm so I can use it as a pillow.

'Imagine if you had to spend your whole life not reading, not going near books,' I say, and he shakes his head and says he doesn't want to imagine it.

'What can I do to help?' he asks.

'Distract me.'

'I can do that. I'm very distracting.'

'You are,' I say, and move in closer to him. 'What's your plan? The life plan for after you sell the bookstore?'

'There are several. I could go to college. Become a lawyer or maybe a literature professor.'

'You've never wanted to be a literature professor. You've always wanted to work in the bookstore.'

'I'll be poor, like my dad.'

'Your dad's got two great kids and a bookstore. He might not be rich but he's not poor.'

'Mum left him. He's working all day every day, trying to hunt down first editions so we can stay afloat. It seems like a hard life.' He shifts around. 'Books can't buy your girlfriend a good night out.'

They can't buy Amy a good night out, he means. 'You know the best night out I've ever had? Hands down the best night? The time you read me "The Love Song of J. Alfred Prufrock".'

'I seem to remember you saying you hated poetry,' he says. 'I distinctly remember you saying something along the lines that poetry is pointless. That we could lose all the poets from the world and no one would care. In fact, thousands of people would be very happy.'

'That's not the argument I was making. You're twisting what I said.'

'What did you say, then? I can't remember.'

'I said poets and poetry don't make a difference to the *real* things.'

'The real things?'

'Words can't save people from cancer or bring people back from the dead. Novels can't either. They don't have a practical use, that's what I meant. I loved that you read the poem to me that night, but the world remained unchanged.'

'And yet you don't think I should sell the bookshop.'

'My theory isn't perfect,' I say, already in the blue that hits before sleep.

I wake in the early morning, with Henry's arm slung around me, and Lola tapping on the window. I open the door and see she's still in the clothes she was wearing last night. She was here for Henry, I guess, but when she sees me, she grabs me around the neck and holds on tight. 'Breakfast?' she asks.

We go next door to Frank's. It's seven. I haven't been up this early for the longest time. It's cool, but the thin yellow light promises a hot day. We order coffee and toast and take a seat at a booth.

'Big night?' I ask, and point at her clothes.

She tips a heap of sugar into her coffee and stirs. 'We played till three. Then Hiroko and I went out to eat. Two gigs to go till we're gone.'

'You should record all your songs,' I tell her as Frank brings our food. 'Make a permanent record of everything you've ever written from start to end.'

'I don't know if I want to record the end,' she says, buttering her toast. 'I'll think about it. So, I saw you and Henry lying together on the floor.'

'We're back to being friends.'

'You two were never just friends,' she says. 'You were inseparable till Amy arrived.'

'Even if I did like him, there's nothing I can do.'

'Tell him.'

'I told him.'

'Tell him to his face and hang around to see what happens. Maybe it works out different this time.'

'What about you and Hiroko?' I ask. I've always wondered if there was anything between them. '*You're* inseparable.'

She goes quiet and thinks about it. 'We're not girlfriends,' she says. 'She's the only person I can write with. We're collaborators. Think of all the songs we wouldn't have if Mick Jagger and Keith Richards never wrote together.'

'You should record your songs,' I say again. 'Sell them at your last show.'

She licks some jam from her thumb, and I can tell she's still sad about Hiroko leaving but she doesn't hate my idea.

I drive home to shower and change. Rose has left a note for me on the kitchen bench.

*I saw you yesterday, walking straight out of the
ER. I was about to come after you but I saw Gus.
Is something wrong? Call if you need me to come home
today. P.S. Your mum called. There's a message from her
on the answering machine.*

I press the button and listen to Mum talking about Gran and Sea
Ridge and her new classes at school. She says she's planning a trip
to the city soon. 'I miss you,' she says, in a voice that's flat and
sad. I delete the message and take a shower.

Henry's behind the counter when I return. I take the coffee cup
that he offers and sit with him to drink it. Michael joins us after
a while, along with Martin and George and Frederick and Frieda.
Sophia arrives with croissants, which makes two breakfasts I've
had this morning.

I ask Michael if we can close the Letter Library for the duration
of the cataloging. 'It's too hard to record comments if people are
looking at the books,' I tell him, and it becomes clear that Sophia
didn't know about the job that Michael's asked me to do.

'Why?' she asks him.

'My reasons are no longer your concern,' he tells her, and gives
me permission to close the Library.

I tape a notice to the front window – THE LETTER LIBRARY IS
CLOSED FOR CATALOGING. HOWLING BOOKS IS SORRY FOR THE IN-
CONVENIENCE – and then start work.

I'd lose all sense of time if it weren't for George and Martin, who keep walking over to put notes in *The Broken Shore*. I've
decided the restriction on the Letter Library doesn't apply to staff,

so I don't say anything. At first George shyly places her letters in the book, but by the last one she's angrily shoving paper in there.

To give her some privacy, I concentrate on recording the notes in *Prufrock and Other Observations*. It takes a long time to record everything that's written, and in the end I have to leave some small notes out. Stranger after stranger has made notes in the margins, circled words, and underlined ideas.

From what I can work out, the poem that Henry read to me that night is the love song of someone who doesn't think very much of himself. He's a man debating whether or not he should tell a woman how much he wants her. The notes in the margins are mostly from people who are worrying that life's passed them by. Or, to quote Henry, people who feel a little bit shit about themselves.

'Is that why you like it?' I ask Henry when he's on a break.

'I think you'll find a lot of people like Eliot for reasons other than that they feel a little bit shit about themselves. Read the language. It's beautiful.'

'But it's basically about him wanting sex, isn't it?'

'I think he's debating whether or not to take a risk.'

Henry stays with me this afternoon to help and to argue further about Eliot. There are so many comments in the book that my hands are tired, so I read them and Henry types. Eventually we get to the last one and Henry walks back to the counter.

I'm too tired to start in on cataloging another book. I proofread what I've done today, and make sure it's formatted. Then I save the database and shut down the computer. Martin's not ready to go yet, so I pass the time looking through the books. The one I really want to look at is Mark Laita's *Sea*. It's one of the most beautiful books I've ever seen; I can't believe someone would leave a copy in the Letter Library for people to write over.

I take it off the shelf today. The creatures are hypnotic, glowing off the pages in brilliant light. I sit on the floor and look through it. I stop when I get to the page with the North Pacific octopus, a red spectacular creature, no eyes that I can see, the end of its body a mouth, open in a kind of blind wonder. There's a tiny arrow pointing to the creature and three words next to that, written in small, neat letters, the kind of letters that Cal used: *this I love.*

Without a doubt, it's Cal's handwriting. I know from the way the tail of his *e* kicks upward. I know it because he loved the octopus. I know because he loved this book. I know it in a way I can't prove. It doesn't make me sad, exactly. It's a feeling I can't seem to name.

I think about it for the rest of the week, and by Sunday I decide the feeling has something to do with Cal being in a library along with other people who no longer exist in the world. The traces of them are hidden, small lines in books. In a library from which no one can borrow.

The Broken Shore

by Peter Temple

Letters left between pp. 8 and 9
January 16–January 22, 2016

Hi Martin, it's George here.

I'm writing to explain some things about last night. I
was wrong about you – you're a nice guy. I liked talking
to you in the bathroom. I liked hearing about your dog
named Rufus that's no particular breed that you know of.
I like that you chose him because he was the strangest
dog at the shelter and you thought no one else would
take him. I meant what I said – I'd like to meet him one
day. I'd like to meet your mums, too, and your little sister.
I think you'd make a great human rights lawyer. I like
that you like mysteries. I like you.

And the kiss – what we had of it – was nice.

But, there's that guy I told you about. I know that he's
stopped writing because he's gone overseas, so I'm going
to wait for him to get back. I'm really hoping that we can

be friends. *It'll be a long summer in the bookstore if we
can't be.*

                                                    George

Dear George,

Thanks for your letter. I still feel like a bit of an idiot,
but your explanation helps. (My kiss was nice?? That's
hugely flattering, thanks, George.) You have my word
that I won't try to kiss you again and yes we can be
friends. I'd like that. I'd like it if we could be friends when
we go back to school, too.

It'll be a long summer if we're not friends, but it'll be
an even longer year.

                                                    Martin

Dear Martin,

Thanks for your reply. That's a huge relief. I meant
it was really nice. It was more than nice. You're a good
kisser. Sure, we can be friends when school starts, but
that might cause some trouble for you with Stacy and
her group.

                                                    George

Dear George,

Friends it is, then. At work and at school. You know, you really need to stop worrying about what people think. That's half your problem.

Martin

Martin,

I have a problem?? You're the one who's hanging out with Stacy, a girl who likes to call people freaks.

George

Dear George,

I'm sorry. I wrote that last note in a bit of a hurry at the end of my lunch break. I didn't mean you had a huge problem, just that you tend to hang out alone at school, and I know of at least one person who's tried to talk to you (me!) and you haven't exactly been friendly. I just meant that you're a great person and maybe the guy you like would have told you who he was before now if you'd been a bit more welcoming.

Martin

Dear Martin,

Fuck off and stop writing to me.

George

Dear George,

　　I'm not fucking off. I'm your friend. Friends don't fuck off. And by the way, friends don't tell each other to fuck off, either.

　　　　　　　　　　　　　　　　　Martin

Martin,

　　Fuck. Off.

　　　　　　　　　　　　　　　　　George

Henry

Martin walks over to me around four on Friday the twenty-second. I know it's the twenty-second of January because I'm staring at the calendar and Tom, our customer who pretty much lives in the Supernatural section, is trying to get me to flip the page with my mind. I stop testing my psychic abilities because Martin looks the closest to angry that I've ever seen him. 'Your sister,' he says, holding up a note, 'just told me to fuck off.'

'She tells me to fuck off all the time,' I tell him. 'I wouldn't take it too seriously.' I share with him the truth that's universally acknowledged in our family – that we're shit at love – and he says, 'I'm not trying to *love* her. I'm just trying to be her friend.' He walks away to vent his frustrations on the cataloging.

I've been having a difficult few weeks myself when it comes to girls. Amy replied to my letter last week with a cryptic text:

Thanks. That means a lot at the moment, Henry.

She hasn't sent anything since and I can't stop wondering what *at the moment* means.

I've also spent the last two weeks trying to cheer up Rachel, but I don't know what to say. I can't do anything obvious, since I'm not allowed to tell anyone about Cal. The only thing I can think of to do is to try to talk to her about it, but she's told me straight out that words won't change anything and she doesn't want to talk.

She's not being rude anymore. She's being what I'd describe as obsessive, and that was *before* she found Cal's note on our copy of *Sea*. Now she's a step beyond obsessive. She's working without breaks, searching, although she hasn't said, for another word from her brother.

Frederick walks over to the counter to check on the state of the Walcott search. I don't have anything to report, but while he's here I ask him a hypothetical question. 'If you had a friend who was upset about, say, a death in the family, but they didn't seem to want sympathy, what would you do? If you thought they needed to talk about it, but they won't talk about it.'

'I think you have to respect their wishes. If they don't want to talk about it, you can't force them.' His eyes move toward Rachel and back to me. 'You could try to make her laugh.'

I used to make Rachel laugh just by being in the same space as her. Now she's got this permanent scowl on her face, which is starting to scare the customers. Not that it matters if she does that. George scares them too.

I keep working, and I think about what I'd write to Rachel, if I wrote to her. After a while, Frederick comes over again and says, 'I think that I would try to be brave. Be myself and talk about the things that people might be afraid to talk about. Death is something we shy away from, except in literature or television, when we tend to stare right at it.'

In the quiet of the afternoon, I write a letter to Rachel. I take Frederick's advice and try to be brave and honest, which I hope is normal for me. Or at least semi-normal. I don't try to make her laugh. It seems disrespectful. I tell her that I've been feeling sad about Cal, which might not be right, but it's the truth.

When Rachel's next door at Frank's, I walk over to the Letter Library. I'd intended to put the letter in the *Prufrock,* but her copy of *Cloud Atlas* is sitting next to her bag, so I leave my letter between pages 6 and 7. I put the book on her seat so she can't miss it.

I go to Frank's for a celebratory Danish and when I get back her copy of *Cloud Atlas* is on the shelves of the Letter Library, face out. I wait until she's gone and then I walk over, hoping that I'll find a letter.

Cloud Atlas

by David Mitchell

Letters left between pp. 6 and 7
January 22–January 29, 2016

Dear Rachel,

I hope you don't mind me writing this letter. I know
you came to the city to forget about Cal, but I can see
you're still thinking about him every second – how could
you not think about him?

This will probably sound stupid to you, but I'm having
trouble believing that he's dead. Maybe I'd be able to
believe it if I'd gone to the funeral, or I'd seen his body.
But in my memories, he's alive, so I can't make my brain
compute the information that I'll never see him again.

This isn't sympathy, Rachel. Or, it's a bit of sympathy,
but it's mostly an observation. You look sad a lot of the
time. But sometimes you look confused. Like you can't
compute the information, either. I hate the thought that

you might forget and remember, forget and remember. I think that must be exhausting.

I wish I'd been there at the funeral. I wish I'd been a good friend. You have my phone number, any time you require me to carry you home in a storm.

I know you've said that words won't bring Cal back, and of course that's true. But if you want to write, you can leave a letter in Cloud Atlas (there's another copy in the Letter Library), between pages 6 and 7. I'll always write back.

Henry

Dear Henry,

Thank you for the letter. I appreciate you writing and the offer to talk.

But honestly, everyone's always telling me to talk and it doesn't do much good. Like I said - words don't bring Cal back.

Rachel

Dear Rachel,

I get it, I do. You know where to find me if something changes.

Henry

Dear Rachel,

OK, I said I get it and I do, but I don't agree with you. I'm sitting in the bookshop tonight. Everyone's gone home and I'm thinking about the point of words. I've actually been thinking about the point of them since you dismissed all poetry three years ago, and dissed all the poets.

'I love you, let's kiss, let's have sex.' I've found those words to be very useful over the years. Presumably you told Joel that you loved him and found them quite useful too. I know you told Cal you love him. Those words mean something, Rachel.

Henry

Dear Henry.

Yes, I told Joel that I loved him and I definitely told Cal. I still tell him every day. But I meant that words are useless in the big scheme of things.

Rachel

Dear Rachel,

Doesn't love fall somewhere in the big scheme of things? Isn't it the biggest scheme?

Henry

Dear Henry,

You know what I mean. I mean words don't stop us from dying. They don't give us the dead back. Death is the biggest in the big scheme of things.

Rachel

Dear Rachel,

I think you've got your schemes the wrong way around. Life is the big scheme; death is the little one at the end.

I think we should go out dancing tonight. It's Friday. We'll invite George and Martin.

Henry

Dear Henry,

Death isn't little. If you think it is, you haven't seen it. But yes. I'll dance with you. Let's go somewhere no one knows us. I've seen you dance. I'm having dinner with Rose tonight. I'll meet you in front of Laundry at nine. We can watch the Hollows, then go somewhere new after that.

Rachel

Henry

Martin and I meet outside Shanghai Dumplings that night. He asks where George is and I have to break it to him that she's not coming. 'It's just you and me, as it turns out.'

'I thought it was a family tradition,' he says.

'I did too,' I say, and try not to sound unhappy about it. This will have to do, but it's a poor substitute for the whole family.

While we wait for Mai Li to seat us, I think about the conversation that Dad and I had earlier. 'Friday-night dumplings is canceled for a while,' he said. 'I'm not in the mood for it and neither is your mother. George has gone to eat at her place tonight, and I'm eating with Frederick and Frieda.'

He took some money out of petty cash so I could pay for Martin's dinner, and gave it to me along with a book he'd bought for me during the week.

The book is a Penguin Classics edition of Jorge Luis Borges's short stories. There are butterflies on the cover, squarish wings fitting together to make a hexagon shape. Some butterflies are breaking off from the whole. 'Read "Shakespeare's Memory",' Dad told me tonight, and I promised him I would.

Dad introduced me to Borges's short stories one night in Year 10 when I was looking for something interesting to read. He put a copy into my hands, and told me to read 'The Library of Babel.' I read it with the dictionary beside me. I only sort of understood the thing. It was full of mathematical and scientific references that I wanted to discuss with Rachel, but she'd left by then. I decided it was about people needing the answers to the world, to the universe, and going mad trying to find them.

Mai Li comes over and I explain it's just the two of us, so she seats us at a tiny table near the restroom. People keep hitting the back of my chair with the door. There's no room for my elbows on the table. There's barely room for the menu, which I look at for the first time in my whole life because I have to decide what to order for one.

It doesn't seem right to talk about books without the family here, but it doesn't seem right not to, so I tell Martin briefly about the Borges that Dad gave me tonight. I hand it over so he can look at it. I try to explain 'The Library of Babel' to him, but I can't really put it into words. 'Rachel would have been able to explain it better.'

'You like Rachel,' he says, and I think about Rachel and me, about how long I've known her, about all the things I know and want to know. I think about the letters we've been writing this week and how much I've been looking forward to the next one.

'She's the closest friend I have.' I'm not sure if 'friends' really covers us.

I take back the book and ask Martin how things are going with

George. I'm surprised when he says things are better. They don't seem better. 'Around this time last week she was telling you to fuck off.'

'And I told her, respectfully, that I had decided not to fuck off,' he says.

'And?'

'And she told me, respectfully, that if I didn't fuck off, she would.'

'I'm confused about how things are better,' I say.

'I was nice to her all week and this afternoon there was a breakthrough. I think we might be friends again.'

Before I can ask him what the breakthrough was, exactly, Martin changes the subject. 'How are things with Amy?'

I realize I haven't thought much about her since I started writing to Rachel this week. I've been thinking about her and Cal. I've known him as long as I've known Rachel. When he was a kid, he followed me around asking me questions, and when he turned twelve he turned into this super brain and the dynamic shifted. I miss him.

'Do you know anyone who's died?' I ask Martin, and he tells me his grandmother. We stop talking to order and then I lean in and ask the question that's been bugging me since Rachel told me the news. 'Where do people go? I mean they're here and then they're not. I can't get my head around it.'

'Did someone you know die?' Martin asks.

'Forget it. Let's talk about something else,' I say, and he immediately drops the subject and we spend the rest of dinner talking about crime fiction and politics and his upcoming Year 12 texts and whether or not fried wontons are better than steamed.

. . . .

It's easy hanging out with Martin, so when we get outside and he points to a poster advertising Pavement, a club not far from here, I agree to go with him for a while. There's time before I meet Rachel, and Pavement isn't the kind of place a guy like Martin should go to alone.

It's walking distance from Shanghai Dumplings. It takes us about ten minutes. When we arrive, there's a line filled with a lot of angry-looking people. I think I saw the club listed at the top of the Most Violent Places in Gracetown in the local paper.

The line moves. We pay our money and get our wrists stamped. I'm kind of hoping Martin gets asked for ID and we can't go in, but he doesn't. We just sail right on through. We walk all the way over to the side of the room. There's a live band that threatens to eat tiny animals onstage and everyone claps at the suggestion. 'Put your back against the wall,' I tell Martin, who's looking around like he's expecting to see a friend. He watches two guys walk past us; one of them is leading the other one by a chain. 'It's really best not to stare, Martin,' I say.

After a while, he leans over and yells in my ear. 'When will George be here?'

'What?' I yell back.

'George. When will George be here?'

'George wouldn't be caught dead in a place like this,' I say, looking around. 'As we speak, George is probably back from Mum's place and playing a nice quiet game of Scrabble with Dad.'

Martin nods and says, 'Riiiiight,' like something's just become clear to him.

Something's just become clear to me, too. 'George told you she'd be here. That was the breakthrough this afternoon?'

'I brought her a coffee in to work all week, and those donuts she likes. Is it unreasonable to think that if a person drinks the coffee and eats the food you buy them, that you're on the way to being friends?'

'This is not unreasonable,' I tell him.

'So this afternoon I asked her if she wanted to maybe meet up somewhere, and she said she might be at Pavement.'

It'd be one thing for George to have said she might be at Laundry and then not turn up. But to tell Martin to come here and wait for her is a shitty move. As much as it pains me to say it, I tell Martin it might be time to start looking for another girl.

'Come to Laundry with me. I'll buy you a beer while we wait for Rachel.'

'I'll just get a taxi and go home,' he says, and he's deflating more and more by the minute. I'm not leaving him alone here, so I sling my arm around his shoulders and walk him to the door.

We leave Pavement and head toward Laundry. 'How long do I have to pay?' Martin asks. 'I'm mean, how hard does a guy have to work to be friends with your sister?'

I'm starting to wonder this myself. I know George had some trouble at school, and that's not her fault. But she's throwing away the chance to have a good friend by her side for her whole final year. 'All I can tell you is I feel certain she's worth it.'

As I say this, I see Amy ahead. She's leaning against a building, not far from the bookshop. My heart still goes crazy when I see her. All she has to do is turn up and I'm back where I started.

'I'm waiting for Greg,' she tells me.

I want to ask her what 'at the moment' meant because 'at

the moment' sounded hopeful. Before I have time to say anything, Greg pulls up and steps out of the car. 'Stop hassling Amy,' he says.

I ignore him and keep talking to Amy. 'What does *at the moment* mean, exactly?'

'Did you hear me?' Greg asks, but I keep my back to him and keep talking to Amy.

'Are you OK?' I ask.

'I think you should go,' she says. 'We can talk later.'

'We're talking now,' I say.

'Did you hear me?' Greg says again, this time loudly in my ear.

'No. Because my ears are not tuned to the frequency of *dickhead*,' I say, turning around to see four guys, all of whom I know from school, each one of them a dickhead.

'Maybe your ears *should* be tuned to the frequency of dickhead,' Greg says, and Amy laughs, which makes him even angrier than he was a second ago.

There isn't much time, just enough to make a lunge at the guy who's taken hold of Martin. 'Run,' I yell, but Martin stays where he is. It's a brave move. Stupid, sure. But brave.

They haul him toward the car first, throw him in the backseat, and slam the door. They grab me next. It takes all of them to pick me up and shove me in the trunk. The last thing I see is Amy standing on the pavement, looking at me.

The car starts, and I feel the rhythm of the road beneath me. It's an understatement to say that the night is not turning out how I imagined. I feel the vibration of the tires on the road coming up from the trunk, and I wish I were the kind of guy who didn't panic but I am not that guy. I'm the guy who panics quite a bit. They won't kill us. They'll do something bad, though, and at this point I think it's best not to imagine it.

All the while I'm lying here, I'm thinking about how Amy could be with this guy. I'm trying to interpret the expression that was on her face before they closed the trunk. Anger at Greg? Horror? Pity for me? Fear?

Surely she can't be even a little bit in love with Greg now. What is there to be a little bit in love with? Part of me is happy he threw me in the trunk and she saw it because there's no way she'll be able to stay with him after tonight. Love's insane. But surely it's not *fucking* insane.

I try to work out which way we might be going based on the speed of the car. First they move slowly because High Street's full of traffic on Friday night, and then it seems like they're weaving through streets. The car picks up speed for a while, and I get the feeling they've taken us across the city to the harbor.

It's about fifteen minutes before they stop. One of them opens the trunk, but Martin's putting up a good fight, so he pushes it back down to help the others. I stop it locking at the last minute. I'm free but I can't run. I'm not leaving Martin, but anyway, there's nowhere *to* run.

I was right. We're on a stretch of road on the other side of the city, near the docks. I can see the packing crates behind us, and a double-lane freeway in front. There are a few warehouses spread out along the road on the other side, but that's about it. No one's finding us. If they tie us up, we could be here all night.

There's just enough time to send a dropped pin to Rachel and a *help!* message before I'm lifted out of the trunk. Martin's taped to a streetlight. They've used duct tape and they haven't been stingy with the amount. He's wrapped up tight. He's also naked. His clothes are in the car, I guess, along with everything else he was carrying.

They do the same thing to me. They make me strip by threatening to kick Martin if I won't, and even though he's in the background saying, 'Kick me. I don't care,' in a defeated voice, I take off my clothes.

In less than ten minutes I'm duct-taped, naked, to the other side of the streetlight and they've filmed the whole thing. I'm fairly certain Greg is the kind of guy with a great internet plan, so we'll be online before they're pulled out from the curb and on to the road.

Once Greg's finished filming, he says I can find myself on YouTube under 'dickhead' and picks up my clothes along with my wallet, my mobile phone, and the bookshop keys. When I yell to him that this turns a prank into a violent assault and robbery, he throws all our valuables on the ground and gets in the car and drives off with our clothes.

'I really dislike Greg Smith. I mean I *really* dislike him.'

'Well, I think the feeling's mutual,' Martin says.

'What kind of guy does this to another guy?' I ask Martin.

'The kind of guy who's getting another guy back for squirting water over his new suit?'

'Is it really the same thing?' I look down at myself. 'This seems worse.'

'It is,' Martin says. 'I'm just saying that you should try to keep a low profile from now on.'

'I sent a dropped pin to Rachel, so she knows our location,' I tell him. 'We just have to wait.'

'Excellent,' he says.

'On a scale of one to ten, how angry with me are you?'

'I'm naked and duct-taped to a pole. That's what I am. That is an accurate description of my feelings. It's not your fault. I just want to concentrate on how we get free.'

People drive past and don't stop. I don't hear car horns, so I don't think they even notice us. Or maybe more people get tied naked to poles by dickheads than you'd think. 'At least it's warm,' I say.

'You're such an optimist,' Martin answers.

'I find it helps to be, considering the regular shitness of life.'

'Why isn't George an optimist?' he asks. 'The guy I told you about has been writing to her through the Letter Library for *three* years and she's almost certain she knows who he is and she's certain she likes him, so why hasn't she done anything about it?'

Three years is a long time to write to someone. That's commitment. That's romantic. I think about George sitting in the window of the shop, acting cynical about love, when all the while she's falling for a secret admirer.

'He might not be who she thinks he is. He might be a psychopath,' Martin says.

'All the psychopaths are on the internet now,' I tell him.

'*Why?*' he asks.

'More potential for victims, I guess.'

'No, why wouldn't George want to meet him? If she really is so sure who he is?'

'She's scared,' I say. 'She's shy.'

'She doesn't seem shy. She seems hostile and aggressive.'

'It's a cover,' I tell him, working something out about my sister in this second.

'Good cover,' Martin says, but I think he's worked it out too because some of the anger's gone out of his voice.

I look around for Rachel's Volvo, wondering if my text got through.

'With a bit of luck, Amy might have called the police,' Martin says.

I love Amy, flaws and all, but I know, without a doubt, that she won't be calling the police. I know she didn't call them after they shut me inside the trunk. She didn't take down the license plate number like Rachel would have. She didn't get in a taxi and say, 'Follow that car.' It's Rachel who we're waiting for. Rachel who's coming to save us.

Pride and Prejudice

by Jane Austen

Notes written on title page

Where's my Mr. Darcy?

He lived in the 1800s, so he's dead, right?

He's a character in a book; he can't be dead.

If he's a character in a book, it's pretty sad for you to like him.

Fuck you.

You can't write *fuck you* on *Pride and Prejudice*. It's a classic.

Who are you?

Who are you? Except for desperate.

You're writing in the book. You're answering me. Who's desperate?

I don't mind the book. I just mind people setting up a character in a book as the perfect guy.

I never said he was perfect. He's flawed.

And you're looking for a flawed guy?

I could be. Who are you?

Albert Finnegan. According to my ex-girlfriends, I am full of flaws.

I'm one of your ex-girlfriends, Albert. I know you're full of flaws.

Jennifer?

The one and only. You never told me you'd read this book.

I've read many books. If you let me speak, you'd know.

Tuesday, August 7, 2010. School cafeteria at 2.

For?

For conversation about Pride and Prejudice.

Rachel

The cataloging stopped being boring as soon as I started the 'Prufrock'. Even the small lines that mean nothing to me must have meant something to someone, so I'm careful to document them. When I'm tempted to skip some, I think about Cal's markings on *Sea* and I don't.

I find a lot of people in the Letter Library this week. Even in the nameless lines I read stories. Pablo Neruda is very sexy. One person has gone through with a hot-pink pen and highlighted what I'm pretty sure are all the references to sex. I could feel that small circle of blush behind my ears going wild when I read it.

That circle's been flaring every time I see a letter from Henry in *Cloud Atlas*. The letters aren't romantic. They're about words and death, mostly, but I like getting them. I love getting them. I go on breaks so I can come back and find one. If I go on a break and there isn't a letter when I get back, I'm disappointed.

I've wanted to talk to Henry more and more with every letter.

I don't know whether I like him again, or if I'm just looking for distraction, or if the love letters I'm finding in the Library are setting off some kind of madness.

On Monday I started reading a series of letters written from A to B in *The Fault in Our Stars*. At first the writers don't call themselves A and B. At first they're just lines on a page, written in different-colored pens. A writes in blue. B writes in black. They write underneath each other: *Funny,* A writes near a particular sentence. *Bloody hilarious,* B writes underneath. By page 50 they're telling each other their favorite lines. By page 100 A says he's a guy and B says he's a guy too. By page 150 it's pretty clear they both like each other. They met, according to the last page of the book, out in front of a club called Hush, on January 2, 2015.

I've gone home every night this week thinking about A and B, thoughts that lead to Henry, which are thoughts that, I have to admit, keep me awake. The only way I've been able to sleep is by distracting myself with *Cloud Atlas*. Whenever I've thought about kissing Henry, I've read a page. It's 544 pages long. I've almost finished the book.

I've run out of distractions, so today, when Henry asked me out dancing, I gave in. My answer was yes.

I drive Martin home and lift the ban on talking because I like Martin but also because he and Henry talk, and I'm wondering if one of the things they've talked about is me. I can't ask him directly, but I'm hoping he'll spill something by accident.

We talk about the cataloging at first. Martin's finding things in books too, but not like I am. He's finding things people leave behind by mistake, the accidental histories of people.

Mostly, we talk about George on the way home this afternoon. He fills me in on what happened after the party. 'She wrote me a letter saying sorry and we made up and then I blew it by telling her she had a problem. But then I bought her coffee and snacks and we made up again.'

He smiles and does this double punch in the air that reminds me of Cal. 'So I asked her if maybe she wanted to meet up tonight and she said yes. We're meeting later after I have dumplings with Henry. Just as friends, of course.'

'Of course,' I say.

He looks so excited that I feel like I should say something to him. If it were Cal next to me about to go out 'as friends' with the girl he liked, I'd tell him to be careful. I don't tell Martin that, though. It's not like I'm being careful about my feelings for Henry.

I'm smiling as I walk into the restaurant, an Italian place not far from the warehouse. I'm thinking about Henry and A and B in *The Fault in Our Stars* and pasta, and then I see Mum sitting next to Rose. 'Surprise,' Mum says in a voice that sounds flat. 'I missed you so much I took the day off school.'

I kiss her on the cheek, and she tells me I smell nice. 'Rose lent me her perfume.'

'You look happy,' Mum says, and maybe I'm imagining it, but it sounds like an accusation, just a soft one.

'I'm actually starving,' I say, reaching over to take a piece of bread.

'I'm glad,' she tells me, and I can see she is, but I can see she's not at the same time. I offer around the bread and Rose fills in the quiet by saying she's heard great things about the restaurant.

'Excuse me,' Mum says before she walks outside for a cigarette.

'She's mad at me,' I say, and Rose looks genuinely surprised.

'Why would she be mad at you? You're all she's talked about since she arrived. But she made the mistake of meeting me at the ER.'

I look through the window at Mum and wonder if we ever just go forward. 'Does it bother you? Don't you think about Cal all day long, with the machines beeping and the people dying?'

'I don't think about Cal there, no.'

'So you get used to it?' I say. 'Used to death?'

'No,' she says, pouring a glass of wine and thinking about it. 'I guess it's that no two deaths are the same. It'd be terrible if they were.'

Rose changes the subject by quizzing me about the bookstore. I focus on her questions so I don't stare at Mum after she comes back to the table. I tell them about the Letter Library and how Michael wants me to catalog it before they sell. 'It's probably too early for offers.'

'It'll go quick,' Mum says, and Rose agrees the building is fantastic, and Mum shakes her head and says, 'They won't keep the building. They'll knock it down to build flats. All around here flats are going up. Behind you at the warehouse, there's another lot.'

It's not Mum's fault that the plan is to knock down the shop, but I'm annoyed that she mentioned it. The Mum who existed before Cal was relentlessly optimistic, she made the best of things, she swam.

'Have you told people, about Cal?' Mum asks.

'I told Henry. I'm not planning on telling anyone else, though, just in case either of you runs into Sophia.'

I'm expecting Rose to argue with me, but she says she can't say the words either. 'Stupid, but I've only told my boss at St. Albert's. I don't want to think about it at work.'

The food arrives, and Mum says Gran wants to know if I've gone through the box of Cal's things that she gave to me before I left.

'It's still in the car,' I tell her. 'I'll get to it, though.'

I think back to that family in the waiting room. I describe them to Rose, and she nods, she remembers them. 'It was the girl's father,' she says. 'He'd been in a car accident.'

'And?'

'And he was OK,' she says, and Mum breathes out in relief.

It makes me feel better that she cares about that unknown family. Somehow it means that even though Cal's death has changed both of us, it hasn't changed us at our core. Mum and I were both there at the moment that Cal died, and sometimes I worry that seeing that has altered something so fundamental about us. Sometimes I worry we lost some of our humanness that day, and it's not coming back. It's hard to deny we're harsher people without him, I think, watching Mum go out for another cigarette.

Toward the end of dinner, I get a text from Henry

–help!–

and a dropped pin on a map showing me his location.

While I'm reading it, Mum and Rose are talking about the three of us having a movie night. Popcorn, chocolate, pillows on the floor. 'I have to go,' I tell them, and I'm relieved that I have a reason to escape, and I'm relieved that I don't have to tell Mum I can't be with her because I'm going dancing. It's not that I'm going out to have fun. 'Henry needs me.'

. . .

I call Lola because I'm not driving to the docks alone. Before I even say hello, she jumps in and tells me in a rush that I was right. 'Your idea was perfect. We've pooled our money and my grandmother kicked in and we're renting a friend's studio for a *brilliant* rate so we're recording all our songs, from the first to the last, every song we've ever written, so we can sell those at our last gig and maybe keep selling them after.' She takes a quick breath but not enough so I can speak. 'Are you looking for Henry? I saw him with Amy and Martin earlier, near the bookshop.'

The comment about Amy stings, and I think for a second about deleting Henry's call for help and going home, but it's not like it's all that surprising he's talking to Amy. And he's never said he's fallen out of love with her. Anything between the two of us is all in my imagination.

I fill Lola in quickly, and her voice shifts from excited to worried. 'Tell her we'll reschedule the recording,' Hiroko says in the background. I can tell Lola's not all that keen on the idea, though. 'Ask George to go with you,' Lola says. 'And if she can't, text me, and we'll come.'

I drive to the bookstore, park in front, and text George from the car, letting her know that I need her help with Henry. It's not that late, but she's already in her pajamas – blue ones with clouds – and she hasn't bothered getting out of them.

'Where are we going?' she asks, and I tell her to look at my phone.

She directs me and we drive toward the city. After five minutes or so, she blurts out, 'Martin asked me on a date. I told him I might be at Pavement.'

'Is Pavement the same kind of place it was three years ago?' I ask.

'It's worse,' she says, and then starts defending herself. 'He told me I have a problem. It just made me so angry.'

I almost point out that he bought her coffee and food but I stop myself. I held a grudge against Henry for three years, so I can't judge her. But Pavement?

'I knew it was awful as soon as I did it. I just couldn't make myself take it back.'

She concentrates on the phone as we come out on the other side of the city and get close to the docks. 'Slow down,' she says. 'Henry's somewhere around here.'

It's a stretch of dim road with lights dotted along it. There are no people, just packing crates and warehouses. 'What's he doing out here?' George asks, and I'm wondering the same thing. I start really worrying when we get to the blue spot on the map and he's not there.

I pull over and George studies my phone. I take it from her. 'It's a double highway. He's on the other side.'

I make a U-turn and spot him before she does. He's shining in the darkness; arms pulled back like a suburban Caravaggio. He tries to wave at the car but his arms are taped to his side.

'Oh, shit,' George says, spotting Martin.

I pull up near them. Henry Jones naked is quite a sight. I try not to look like I'm enjoying it as much as I am.

'Hello,' he says after we've climbed out of the car.

'Hello,' I say. 'You seem to have gotten yourself in some trouble.'

'You're naked,' George says.

'Really?' Henry says. 'We hadn't noticed.'

'Why are you naked?' George asks.

'Why are you in your pajamas?' Martin asks as she walks around to his side of the pole.

'I had to leave in a hurry, to save you.'

'Maybe I wouldn't need saving if *someone* hadn't told me she'd be at Pavement tonight.'

'Someone said she *might* be there,' George says.

I decide it's the best thing for everyone if we get Martin and Henry free as quickly as possible. There's nothing in the backseat, so I open the trunk, and there, next to Cal's box, are scissors and, for some reason, a steak knife. I pick them up, and before I close the trunk, I stare at the lid that's taped shut on Cal's box, and I almost open it. George walks over, though, so I close the trunk. 'You free Martin with the scissors. I'll free Henry with the steak knife.'

There's some commentary from Henry about the strangeness of having a steak knife, but as Martin points out, it's a strange kind of night. The steak knife seems the most normal thing.

'Do you have a steady hand?' Henry asks.

'Not particularly,' I say. 'I'll go carefully around the sensitive parts.'

'It's all sensitive, really.'

'You don't look half bad naked,' I say, to lighten the mood.

'I'll take that to mean I look half good.'

'Close your eyes,' I hear Martin say to George. *'Stop looking at me.'*

'Relax,' George says.

'Relax?' he says. 'If you didn't want to be friends, you could have just said so. Do I need to beg every single day? You haven't even bothered to say sorry.'

He yells the last bit, and George doesn't answer for what seems like a long time. Eventually she says, very quietly, 'Sorry.'

'What?' Martin asks. 'You'll have to speak up.'

'I'm sorry,' George says loudly.

'I accept,' says Martin.

'Careful of my penis,' Henry says, and suddenly I find the whole situation hilarious. I haven't found anything funny in ten months. Usually I pretend to laugh. I say something's funny. I try to make jokes. But really, since Cal died, nothing's actually funny. Except tonight, Henry Jones naked in front of me is hilarious.

'Don't laugh while you're cutting,' he says, and for some reason that's funny too.

'You're shaking,' he says, and George is laughing now and Martin is laughing and Henry's saying, 'I'm glad my naked nuts are so hilarious to you all,' but he's laughing too, and he's happy that everyone else is happy, because that's the kind of guy Henry is.

We all pile in the car and Henry and George convince Martin to stay at the bookstore tonight so I don't have to drive across the river. 'You can sleep in my bed,' Henry tells him. 'I'll sleep in the shop with Rachel.'

After Henry and Martin are dressed, we all sit behind the counter and watch the clip on YouTube. 'You really can't see much,' Martin says.

'Of you,' Henry points out. 'There's a fairly shocking close-up of me.' He puts down his phone and decides he doesn't care. 'So people see us naked. So what?'

'So I go back to school in a storm of ridicule,' Martin says.

'I'll be there,' George offers, and he gives her a look that suggests this is a very good consolation prize.

The two of them go upstairs. Henry and I lie on the floor in front of the Letter Library. He turns off the lights so we're just voices in the dimness. 'I worry sometimes that Greg Smith is a better kisser than me, and that's why Amy chose him.'

'Speaking as a girl who's kissed you before, I can reassure you. There's nothing for you to worry about in that department.'

'I'm sorry I don't remember more of it,' he says. 'Was I better than Joel?'

'You were different,' I say.

'Did you have sex with him?'

'That's a personal question.'

'We're best friends. Best friends get to ask personal questions.'

'Did you and Amy have sex?'

'You're right. It is a personal question.'

'Do you still love her?' I ask.

'Do you still love Joel?' he asks.

'Maybe we should talk about something else.'

'Things have changed between us,' he says, but he doesn't say how, and I'm not sure if he means things have changed between him and Amy, or him and me.

'What good things happened, in the last three years?' he asks. 'You've only told me the bad stuff.'

I haven't thought about the good things in a while, but a lot of good happened before Cal died. 'I won the science awards, before Year 12. And the math award. I swam five kilometers every day with Mum. Dad visited and took Cal and me windsurfing. I was sports captain in Year 11. What about you?'

'I won the English prize. I did pretty well in Year 12. I went to the Year 12 dance with Amy. Lola and Hiroko wrote a song about me. I won a short story competition.'

'That's a good list,' I say.

'Can we try again to go out dancing?' Henry asks.

'Yes,' I tell him for the second time.

'I love lying here with you, under the books,' he says.

And then we fall asleep.

The Broken Shore

by Peter Temple

Letters left between pp. 8 and 9
February 1–February 5, 2016

Dear George,

I appreciate all the apologizing, but seriously, you can stop now. So what if everyone in class saw me naked? The shots were mostly of Henry.

If you really want to make it up to me, maybe you could tell me about the letter guy. Who do you think he is?

Martin

Martin,

I know you've told me to stop, but I need to say one last time – I'm sorry. To make it up to you, yes, I'll tell you about the guy, who I think is Cal Sweetie.

I'm not a hundred per cent sure it is him, but before the first letter arrived, he was in the bookshop a lot, and he wasn't just here to talk to Rachel. He spent a lot of time looking through the Letter Library.

He'd tried to talk to me at school, but I hadn't said much back. You're right, OK, I'm a little defensive but I'm the girl reading secondhand books when everyone else has the latest smartphones. I wear secondhand clothes too. My dad comes to parent-teacher interviews and loudly announces to my homeroom teacher that we can't afford to send me to camp.

Let me be clear: I don't care that we're broke sometimes. The bookshop is worth it. But it doesn't pave the way to popularity. It's easier to block people out than hear them call me a freak.

But Cal isn't like that, and I missed out on talking to him at school, and then he left for Sea Ridge with Rachel. The letters kept coming, but I saw Tim Hooper, Cal's best friend, at our book in the Letter Library, and it convinced me even more that the writer was Cal.

I could have told him I knew before now, but I wasn't sure that I liked him that way till he stopped writing. I thought he was kind of geeky and a little strange at first but sometime after his letters stopped, he started to look cute to me. He's sweet. And kind. And I want to meet him face to face and talk.

George

Dear George,

I know Cal a little, and he is all the things that you've written about him. I hope you get to meet him and it works out.

You might think you need to keep people at bay – but if you weren't so reclusive at school, I think you'd actually have a lot of friends. You're interesting and funny. And I very much like your clothes. I very much like everything about you, George.

Martin

Cloud Atlas

by David Mitchell

Letters left between pp. 6 and 7
January 30, 2016

Dear Rachel,

Thank you for saving me last night. You snore, by the way. But it's not an unpleasant sound. It's like a soft nuzzling. When should we dance?

Henry

Dear Henry,

I'm happy to save you anytime. You drool, by the way. But it's a pleasant kind of drooling. When do you want to dance?

Rachel

Dear Rachel,

You steal the quilt - but I don't mind. George and Martin seem to be getting on quite well today. I'm thinking if we wait a week, they'll be getting on even better and they might come with us. Let's dance next Saturday?

Henry

Dear Henry,

Yes.

Rachel

Henry

We decide to dance on Saturday at Bliss, a place with a DJ who, according to Lola, plays a pretty decent mix. I put a big circle around Saturday, February 6, on the bookshop calendar because I'm excited.

The club lets in underage people. If you can show ID on the way in, you get a yellow bracelet. No bracelet, no alcohol. It means George and Martin can come. I didn't have to convince Rachel. I asked her and she said yes.

Rachel and I have been writing letters all week, leaving them in *Cloud Atlas*. Sometimes we don't even bother waiting till the other person is away from the Letter Library. I look at Rachel and she looks back, as I'm sliding the note in the pages.

'It feels sexy,' I whisper to Lola on the train tonight.

Bliss is at the north end of the city, near Parliament Station, so we've left the cars at home. The train is crowded. Rachel and

George sit together. Martin sits in a seat behind them. Lola and I stand in the middle of the car.

'Is that why you look so good tonight?' Lola asks, touching the hem of my shirt.

Honestly, I'm not sure which girl I made an effort for. Amy might be there. Rachel is here.

'Don't fuck Rachel around,' Lola says.

'What's wrong with you?'

'You fucked her around once and she left us both, so what I'm saying is you can't fuck her around again.'

'I ask again, what's wrong?'

'She came over to my place earlier. I cut her hair. Waxed her legs. Lent her some clothes.'

'She looks gorgeous.' She looked gorgeous before.

'I think maybe she wanted to look good for you. But if you go overseas with Amy, which you will if she asks, then where does that leave Rachel?'

'Did she say she wanted to look beautiful for me?'

Lola slaps me softly on the cheek, and I get the message.

We're quiet for a while, and then she says, 'I'm thinking about asking Hiroko to stay.'

Even I, as bad as I am at friendship, know this is a terrible idea. I listen to all her reasons – the more they record their songs, the more Lola knows the Hollows could really be something. 'She doesn't need to study music.'

'She wants to study music. You can't ask her not to go.'

'I could just float the idea,' she says as the train stops, and the door opens and she walks out ahead of me, moving fast to find Hiroko, I guess.

We're all dancing tonight, not drinking, so none of us needs a yellow bracelet. The music's loud. There's no chance of talking. We walk to the dance floor and start moving. I love dancing. It's true I'm no good at it, but it's also true I don't give a shit. Rachel and I gravitate toward each other when Iggy Pop's 'Sister Midnight' comes on. The DJ is classic Lola – all the songs we danced to in her bedroom and in the garage.

Martin and George have gone to sit at a table, so it's just Rachel and me. I yell to fill her in on Lola's plan to ask Hiroko to stay, and although I can't clearly hear the answer, Rachel's expression lets me know she agrees with me – bad idea. Very bad idea.

A slow Radiohead song comes on, and Rachel and I look at each other awkwardly for a second or two, and then I think, fuck it. We're friends. I can dance close to her if I want.

It's easier to talk because my mouth is beside her ear. I tell her I've missed her, and she asks me what specifically I've missed about her.

'I got all my scientific facts from you, for one thing. I'm a total brain because of the information you gave me. Ask me a question. I'll prove it.'

'Name the nine planets,' she says.

She watches me thinking. 'You look like you're in pain.'

'That's my look of absolute genius. You don't have a similar look?'

'I hope not.'

'Well, that probably means you're not an absolute genius. OK. Nine planets: Mercury, Venus, Earth, Mars, Jupiter, Saturn, Uranus, Neptune.'

'That's eight.'

'Thanks to information you gave me in Year 7, I know that

was a trick question. There are only eight planets. Pluto is a dwarf planet.'

'Impressive,' she says. 'You should kiss me.'

'I should name the eight planets more often. Did I hear you right?' I pull back so I'm looking at her face, at her mouth, at her ears and freckles and neck. 'You want to kiss me?'

She points over my shoulder, and I follow the line of her finger and see Amy. 'You really want her back?' Rachel asks, but doesn't wait for my answer. Instead, she loops her hands around my neck. 'Relax. We're just making her jealous,' she says.

And then she leans in and kisses me. For a very long time.

Rachel

I don't intend to kiss Henry.

When I pull him close, it's out of frustration. I saw Amy before he did. She's wearing a killer dress – her hair is perfect. Greg is nowhere to be seen. My guess is she's here to make sure Henry's not going anywhere.

'You really want her back?' I ask Henry, but the answer is in his body. The second he spots her, he turns in her direction. I step in close, and he looks surprised and worried, so I tell him to relax. 'We're just making her jealous.'

It's a good kiss. The first kiss I've really felt in a long time. I'd be lying if I said I didn't feel it in all sorts of places. I keep my eyes closed, but the lights seem to have gotten under my lids, and there's a flickering show happening in the darkness. Thoughts turn in the kaleidoscope, in no particular order – why would Amy keep leaving someone who kissed like this? Cal should have lived to kiss a girl. What is Henry thinking? When should we stop?

I pull away first. I try to read Henry's expression – confused, worried, thrilled – all three maybe. 'Is she still watching?' I ask.

'Yes,' he says, and I can feel his breath as he answers.

'You'll have her back within the month,' I tell him, and try not to sound unhappy.

We don't hang around. I tell Henry it'll be better for the plan if we leave now, and together. I can't see Lola anywhere or George and Martin, so we text to let them know we're leaving.

Henry suggests we walk home. We're less than an hour away, and if we get tired we'll get a taxi. It's a hot night. There are loads of people on the street. This is the time I love the city. I hate it in the day when the air is gray and the heat bounces off concrete.

We walk through the streets without talking, the kiss making things awkward between us. I decide to put him out of his misery. 'It didn't mean anything, Henry. I was helping you out. It's not worth being embarrassed about small things.'

I try to explain what it's like to see your brother on the beach, looking like that, looking *empty*. 'Nothing seems important after that. Or, the small things don't seem important.'

'I disagree,' he says.

'But you don't know what I know,' I say.

'I disagree that love and sex are the small things. I don't need to have seen a dead body to know that I'm right about that.'

We take the shortcut through the park. The sprinklers are on, and we rest near one and hold our legs over the soft sprays of water.

He points to the park light and the moths that are flying around it. 'Why are they doing that?'

I look at the moths, a golden storm around the light, and tell him that they're phototactic. 'Phototaxis is when something automatically moves to or away from light. Moths are positively phototactic – they're attracted to light.'

I look over at him while he's looking up. There's a dusting of freckles but only on the left side of his face and running down his neck, disappearing under his collar.

'No one knows for certain,' I tell him. 'But some people think that migrating moths use the night sky to navigate. They follow the lights in the sky.'

'But they're flying around a streetlight,' he says.

'They've been using the moon as a guide, flying toward it, but never expecting to reach it, and then they hit the light and think maybe that's it.'

'They're pretty far away from the moon,' he says.

'Yeah,' I tell him. 'But they don't know that.'

We sit here for a long time. Henry takes off his shoes and socks to feel the water on his feet. We look at the moths. Henry points out the way the water reflects on the grass, the blackbird singing at night, the shadows of buildings. It's like he's picking up parts of the world and showing them to me, saying, See? It's beautiful.

We get back to the shop around two. George and Martin and Lola took a taxi, so they're home ahead of us. George and Martin are talking in the reading garden. Lola is zonked out on the fiction couch. According to George, Hiroko didn't take Lola ordering her to stay in the country all that well. 'Lola drank a lot of wine very quickly,' Martin says.

I put a glass of water next to her and leave her sleeping.

Henry makes us a quilt bed again. My plan was to go home because at the club tonight I saw the future. Amy will come back to Henry, and he will go back to her, but I can't help myself. I text Rose to tell her I'm staying the night. She texts a winking smile back to me. She'll be disappointed when Henry and Amy get back together.

So will I, but he's already lying on our floor bed, and the thought of talking to him all night appeals. The bookstore appeals, and it has an end date, or it will when they find a buyer, so I decide to make the most of Henry and the store while they're here.

We listen to the sounds of the street and the bookstore. 'Remember how your dad used to tell us the place was haunted?' I ask Henry.

'Secondhand books are haunted, according to him. Ghosts in the pages.'

'You believe in them,' I say.

'I don't disbelieve. *There are more things in heaven and earth, Horatio, than are dreamt of in your philosophy.*'

'*Hamlet?*' I ask.

'Very good,' he says.

'It's underlined in the Library.'

'So maybe there's something to it.'

'I see Cal,' I tell him. 'He's a hallucination but he seems so real. I can actually smell gum.'

'Is that possible?' he asks, and I tell him it is.

'You can hallucinate smells and sounds.'

'And you're sure he's not a ghost? You never thought he might be?'

'I know he's not, but I can't help hoping that he might be. Sometimes a television show will come on, one that he loved, and I'll get so sad, because he'll never know how it ends. And I think, if he's a ghost, then at least he can watch *Game of Thrones*.'

'Maybe there's *Game of Thrones* on permanent stream wherever he is.'

'That's what we think because we can't imagine what it's like to not exist.'

I move a little closer to him, because that thought makes me want to move a little closer. He stretches out his arm so I can lie on it, and it makes the thought of not existing slightly less terrifying.

'You're warm,' he says.

'It's a warm night.'

'Cal believed in them,' he says, and we're back to the ghosts.

'Cal believed in all kinds of things,' I say, and he laughs as if he's remembering those Sunday-night dinners at our place.

'He used to love to mess with my head with his theories of time,' he says. 'Like the block universe theory of time. I still don't understand it.'

'The block universe theory of time states that the past, present, and future are all happening simultaneously,' I say, thinking about that night when Cal was explaining it to us. He'd just read a book about it – *Objective Becoming* by Bradford Skow, who told the reader to imagine time as another dimension, a dimension like space, and then imagine they could see the universe from above, get outside the universe, and look down. If they could do that, then they'd see all the events of their life spread out like they see things in space spread out.

'You think it's true?' Henry asks.

'I've never been outside the universe; I couldn't say.'

Cal thought it was true. At least he liked the idea of it. 'Think of it like this,' Cal had said. 'This house we're in doesn't stop existing just because we leave it, and the past doesn't either.'

'It's a nice thought,' I say.

We're quiet for a while, and then Henry says, 'That would mean if we could get high enough, outside of the universe, we'd see what's in front of us?'

I tell him I could look in the book and find out, but he shakes his head and yawns. 'If my future already exists somewhere, I don't want to know. I want to live under the illusion that I have complete control over my life.'

I want that too. I want to touch the scar I've just noticed on Henry's chin. I want to kiss him again, for real this time. I think I knew when I came back to the city that this moment would come. The moment when I wouldn't feel overwhelmed by sadness for Cal, when I'd feel overwhelmed by Henry.

'If our lives are there, in the future, already mapped,' Henry says, 'then who writes them? Because if the future is set, then someone must plan that future, and with seven billion people in the world, that's impossible. The logistics alone rule it out.'

'You think we're governed by chance, then.'

'I'm convinced of it.'

'I want to believe that. Because if we're not ruled by chance, then Cal was always going to die on that day and he was born with a terrible future.'

Henry tightens his arm around me and says people could go mad looking for the answers. He read a story, by Borges, called

'The Library of Babel'. It was about people looking for the answers, looking for a book that contained them.

'So?' I ask. 'Did they find the answers?'

'The answers don't exist. You know that.'

I tell Henry about Cal's last days, about the reasons I feel so cheated. Looking back, those days leading up to his death were beautiful and thick with meaning. The light felt different. Milk gold. He and I spent more time talking about the future than we'd ever done.

I remember one night he came into my room. He said, 'Shhh,' and waved for me to follow. We went to the water and walked along the edge, and we saw a silver fish, too big for the shallows. We pushed it gently out to sea. The dark velvet-blue and the silver seem unreal to me now, but it happened. I'd never connected it before, but the dream fish must come from that memory, swimming through depths to the surface.

Cal told me the day we saw them that, lately, he couldn't sleep for thinking about all the things he wanted to see – the midnight sun, and its opposite, the polar night, to see the sun stay below the horizon. At one or two in the afternoon to see the light reflected off the sea and the snow, see everything coated in blue.

I tell Henry how we talked our way over the whole world, all the places we wanted to dive – Alaska, the Gulf of Mexico, Malaysia, Japan, Antarctica.

'After, at the funeral, I thought that it was cruel that in the month before he died, he thought so much about the life he wanted to have.'

'I don't know how to talk to you about this,' Henry says, 'because I've never been where you are. But I will be where you are, at some stage in the future, because it's impossible for me not to be. And it seems to me as though you're looking at it the wrong way around.'

He tells me that maybe Cal got lucky. Those last days seemed so beautiful, filled with golden light. 'Maybe he didn't get screwed over by the universe. Maybe it was trying to cram everything in for him.'

'Not very scientific,' I say.

'Sometimes science isn't enough. Sometimes you need the poets,' he says, and it's in this moment, this exact moment, that I fall in love with him again.

Pride and Prejudice and Zombies

by Jane Austen and Seth Grahame-Smith

Letters left between pp. 44 and 45

January 2, 2015

Dear George,

Happy New Year! Did you do anything? I spent the night on the beach with my sister watching the fireworks. We listed our New Year's resolutions (my secret one is that I'm going to try to tell you who I am). I told my sister I'd like to have a girlfriend, which is true. I would like to have a girlfriend, but only if that girlfriend is you. I know you can't agree to that without knowing who I am – I'm working on having the courage.

My biggest fear is that I tell you and you're so disappointed that I never hear from you again. My second biggest fear is that you laugh.

I have to tell you soon because my friend is moving out of town, and this friend has been leaving my letters and collecting yours for me. I moved a while back, but I

never mentioned it because I thought you'd guess who
I was.

Anyway, my sister doesn't have to resolve to have a
boyfriend, because she already has one. Her resolution
is to get her next-level diving certificate. That's one of
mine too. I saw this picture of the underwater canyons
in California. There were all these glowing creatures.
That far under the water, things have to make their own
light because there's nothing, not an inch of sunlight.
William Beebe, this explorer, described the deep as outer
space, which is maybe why I want to go there so badly. It
just looked so beautiful - all that darkness, and all that
drifting light.

Pytheas (name soon
to be revealed)

Dear Pytheas,

I'd like to know who you are - I don't think I'll be
disappointed. I love getting these letters. I wait for them.

I'd like to be your girlfriend. My fear is that when we
meet for real, you won't like me.

George

Dear George,

I won't like you? Never. Gonna. Happen.

Pytheas

Henry

This week is all about distraction and confusion. I spend it thinking of Rachel and waiting for Amy to come back. Rachel assures me every day that it's only a matter of time. 'The kiss will work, Henry. Trust me.' I know the kiss worked. It worked on me.

I distract myself by pumping Martin for information about him and George. 'Nothing's going on,' he keeps saying to me, but that's not true. There's quite a bit of flirting going on. Quite a few letters, too.

'She still likes the other guy,' he says, crouching in front of the nonfiction shelf. 'He's pretty much all we talk about.'

'That's a bit shit,' I say.

'Yes, Henry. That is a bit shit,' he says.

I've been looking in the Letter Library for any clue about the mystery guy, but so far, I've found nothing. The cataloging is really coming along. I distract myself on Tuesday by looking through Rachel's database. There are so many people in the Library, so many people who've left parts of themselves on the pages over the years. I lie next to Rachel sharing lines I love that were marked by strangers.

'*You have been in every prospect I have ever seen since – on the river, on the sails of the ships, on the marshes, in the clouds.*' I read out Pip's speech to Estella, and Rachel tells me that my dad underlined that and dedicated the book to my mum. I turn to the front page and see his writing.

'It's all about Pip, isn't it?' Rachel asks. 'The speech. She's part of him. There's nothing about who she is.'

'My dad's love for my mum isn't all about him, though,' I say, and Rachel tells me that's not what she means.

'It's just something I thought.'

'People's love is always about themselves, though, isn't it?' I ask. 'I mean, pretty much?'

'Maybe. It'd be nice if it wasn't, though.'

'Amy's love is kind of all about her, but I don't really mind.'

'Maybe you should,' Rachel says, and keeps cataloging.

In trying to distract myself from Amy, I'm having other thoughts that I need to distract myself from – Rachel, for one. I've been writing to her to keep my mind off Amy, but the strange thing is that my mind keeps drifting back to the kiss. Drifting back in unsettling ways.

On Wednesday, in an effort to distract myself from Amy and Rachel and Martin and George and Dad's failed Great Expectations, I'm playing a game of Scrabble with Frederick and Frieda. They're playing together against me and we're sitting at the counter, in case customers come in.

'Sometimes kisses are just good,' Frieda says, 'and they don't mean anything.'

Frederick studies the tiles. 'Yes. However, in this case, Henry has known Rachel for a very long time.'

They go into quiet discussion before placing *account* on the board.

'But I like Amy,' I say.

'I don't like Amy,' Frieda says.

Frederick remains neutral.

I look over at Rachel. If she hadn't kissed me, everything would be the same. I just have to forget she kissed me.

To distract myself from the conversation about the kiss, I ask Frederick if Dad's given him any information about the sale. The two of them are good friends. Chances are, Dad will run things past Frederick before he tells us.

'There's some interest. But I don't think your mother and father quite agree.'

'Because the price isn't high enough?' I ask, putting down my tile to form the next word.

'I'm not entirely sure,' he says. 'I think because your father doesn't want to sell to developers.'

'Mum wouldn't sell to developers,' I say, and then there's a run of customers, so I take a break from Scrabble to serve them. Frederick and Frieda keep playing the game, against each other now. By the time I'm done with the customers, they've moved into the reading garden and Lola's taken their place at the counter.

It's the first time I've seen her since I drove her home on Sunday morning. She didn't say much about what happened because she was hungover, but the gist of it seemed to be that Hiroko felt she was being unbelievably selfish for asking her to stay. Considering Lola led into the request with something along the lines of 'You're ruining my life and you'll be nothing without me,' I'm not surprised Hiroko reacted badly.

'Have you spoken to her?' I ask, and Lola shakes her head.

'I know you're on her side,' she says. 'If it didn't involve me, *I'd* be on her side. She says all I think about is music. She says I haven't once thought about her in this. But the only thing I've wanted since Year 9 is the Hollows. I didn't apply to college, and maybe if she'd told me she was applying, I might have.'

'You've never wanted to study music at college,' I remind her. All her life, Lola's had one dream: being on a stage playing her own stuff.

'Are you still playing the last gig on February fourteenth?' I ask.

'I don't know if Hiroko wants to play a last gig with me.'

In an effort to distract Lola from Hiroko, I tell her what I'm trying to distract myself from. 'You know how Rachel kissed me?'

The question shocks her out of unhappiness, momentarily. 'I did *not* know that.'

'You didn't see last Saturday?'

'I don't remember much from last Saturday,' she says. 'But why hasn't she told me since?'

It's an interesting question, and the answer I think is that Rachel actually feels nothing for me and it wasn't worth telling Lola. I stare at the triangle of skin that's showing while Rachel reaches for a book. I'd like to kiss that triangle of skin. 'She said she was doing it to make Amy jealous and help me out.'

'Sure. And pigs fucking fly, Henry. She likes you.'

Cloud Atlas

by David Mitchell

Letters left between pp. 6 and 7
February 10, 2016

Dear Rachel,

I don't think I've thanked you quite enough for the kiss. It's actually the nicest thing a girl has ever done for me.

I've been searching for more Derek Walcott, online, for Frederick this week. I've ordered some in, but I don't get the feeling I've found the right copy, so I'll keep searching. I've been reading my way through an edition of Tennessee Williams's plays. I finished A Streetcar Named Desire last night. Very sexy. Very sad. It made me feel like love is a thing that could fall apart in my hands. Desire, on the other hand, is something that's alive and well. But I know you're not interested in either of those things, being dead on the inside as you say.

I actually think you're the opposite of dead. I think
you're trying to be dead so you don't think about Cal.
Is that why you haven't told anyone but me, yet?

                                        Henry

Dear Henry,

I don't think I phrased it exactly like that - I'm not
completely dead on the inside.

I don't know why I haven't told anyone but you about
Cal. It can't be so that I don't think about him because
I do that all the time.

At the moment I keep going over the week leading
up to his death. This giant bird arrived in town. Cal and
I were sitting on the beach. We'd finished eating fish and
chips and were licking the salt off our fingers when it
landed in front of him.

He held out his last chip, but it wouldn't take it. The
bird stared right at him, with eyes that were different
from any bird eyes I'd seen before.

I didn't like the way it looked at him, or the way it
followed us home, a low gray eyelash on the sky. I didn't
like that it was there when we arrived.

Mum's a crazy birdwatcher, and she was outside with
her books trying to locate the exact species. She studied
the wings and the eyes and the beak and the claws, but
we couldn't pin it down. Its wings were luminescent in the
darkness, like a pearl shot through with the blues and
greens that come out in certain lights.

On the night before Cal died, I saw him outside with the bird. He ran a finger all the way down its chest and it didn't move.

He headed off to the beach, and there was something about his shadow on the lawn; about the way the bird flew above him, an avian moon. The blues and the purples in the night seemed to be swamping him, and when I look back now, I can see that even the light was telling me about what was coming. I think it was a sign. I think that we got so many signs and we ignored them because we didn't believe in them then.

I wonder if the future sends us hints to get us ready, so that the grief doesn't kill us when it comes.

Rachel

Dear Rachel,

I believe in a lot of things that you don't - you know I'm superstitious.

But I don't believe that the future gives us signs. I think that we look back and read the past with the present in our eyes. I think that's what you're doing. Maybe you need to look forward, and start reading the future.

Henry

I text Rachel after dinner tonight, to make sure she's OK. The letters we exchanged this afternoon felt important. I'd call, like in the old days, but she's explained that the warehouse has no walls and Rose works long hours, so when she's home, she needs her sleep.

Me: What are you doing?

Rachel: Finishing *Cloud Atlas*. I liked it. I don't think I completely understood it.

Me: I don't think you're alone.

Rachel: I think it was a novel, though. I think the stories are interconnected. The characters all had that same comet birthmark. Someone's written a note in my copy about the transmigration of the soul – do you believe in that?

Me: What is transmigration, exactly?

Rachel: The passing of a soul, after death, into another body.

Me: I don't know if I believe in it. Do you?

Rachel: No, but it's a beautiful idea.

Me: You're always so certain about things. I wonder how it would feel, to be so certain.

Rachel: You're certain about Amy. You're certain that selling is the right decision.

Me: I'm certain it's the most profitable decision.

Instead of texting back, Rachel calls. She starts in on what she wants to say without even a hello. 'This is important, Henry. I want you to imagine, really imagine, that Howling Books is gone. I want you to imagine that you go to work, every morning, to a normal nine-to-five job. Imagine there's no Frederick and Frieda at the job. No George, no Martin, no me, no Michael, no books.'

'OK.'

'What are you imagining?' she asks.

'I'm sitting at a desk, typing.'

'What are you typing?'

'A letter to you.'

'In this job, you can't type a letter to me. This job doesn't allow for writing in your spare time. Now imagine you have a decent wage. Amy is waiting for you at home. You live in a flat. You sleep in a regular bed.'

I stop imagining. 'I know all this, Rachel. I know life won't be as good without the shop. But I also know the shop won't be around forever. I can't fight the future.'

'The future isn't here yet,' she says, and refers me to my last letter.

Rachel

It's been a strange week. My dreams of Cal have been exchanged for dreams of Henry. It's as though I've traveled back in time to Year 9, when thoughts of him hounded me.

Henry's been distracting himself from thoughts of Amy by talking to me. I decided it wasn't a bad idea, so on Tuesday I found myself texting Joel and asking how he's doing in order to distract myself from Henry.

I'm OK, he replied. I'm better now that I've heard from you.

I felt bad for using him, although I wasn't entirely sure that's what I was doing. I do miss him. The missing started up this week, after the kiss from Henry.

It makes no sense, but when I read Joel's texts, I could almost feel the ocean in them. He was on the beach, looking at the water, and for the first time since I arrived in the city, I wanted to hear its rhythm.

I called Mum after texting Joel to tell her that I'd forgotten the sound of the ocean. She held out the phone, and I knew she was on the beach. I stood in the warehouse, the phone held to my ear like a shell.

'Are you OK?' she asked after a while.

'Yes and no,' I said. 'You?'

'Yes and no,' she said.

'When will it be yes?' I asked, but there's no answer to that, so she held out the phone again and we listened to the waves.

When Henry texts tonight, I almost don't answer. It's dangerous talking to him because it makes me want to talk more and more. I turn off the phone, and then I turn it back on. I look at the text for a while, and then I eventually decide it's rude not to reply.

I text back that I've finished *Cloud Atlas*. I tell him that I think the stories are all connected, but I'm not a hundred per cent sure. I keep staring at the cover, at those pages rising to the sky, and wondering about transmigration of the soul. I don't want to wonder alone.

I stop texting and call him when he sounds uncertain about the bookstore because I know he'll regret selling. All I do is make him angry. He can't change the future, he says, and I think of him and Amy and how much I want him. 'The future isn't set,' I say, and hope that I can make him believe it.

'Henry,' I say, just before he hangs up. 'I want a do-over.'

'A what?'

'A do-over. On the fourteenth of February, this Sunday night. I want to spend another last night of the world together. I want you to promise me that whatever happens with Amy, you won't ditch me for her. The end of the world will be at six in the morning on

February fifteenth. Before then I want to watch Lola and Hiroko play their last song. I want to watch the sunrise.'

'Agreed,' he says. 'And I want to take you book hunting.'

'Agreed,' I say.

'Can I ask you for something else, too?' he says.

'Depends what it is,' I say.

'Tomorrow night is the one Friday night we don't have dumplings so we can host the book club. I want you to be there with me. It might be our last one.'

'Agreed,' I say again, and we hang up.

Great Expectations

by Charles Dickens

Letters left between pp. 508 and 509
February 11, 2016

Michael,

I know how upset you are at losing the bookshop.
I'm upset, too. But ignoring the sale won't change the
situation. As much as we both want the bookshop to do
better, it's not. Can we please talk?

There are developers making very generous offers.
(See the paperwork I left on your desk.) We could also
go to auction. If you won't talk, will you please give me
permission to make all the decisions?

Sophia

Sophia,

Frederick and I have been discussing the sale. Would you consider giving us the time to buy you out?

Michael

Dear Michael,

I wish I could say yes. I know it would make you happy. But have you looked into what the building is worth? See the paperwork left on your desk. Where on earth would you get money like that? I don't want to see you in that kind of debt, and that debt would affect the kids. This is hurting me, too, but please accept reality for Henry and George's sake.

Sophia

Henry

The book club, which we host only in the sense that we supply the books, the wine and the cheese, starts at seven on the second Friday of the month. Before Mum and Dad stopped coming to Friday-night dinners, it was the only Friday that we didn't eat at Shanghai Dumplings.

Dad excuses himself from book club tonight. He helps us set up the food and drink, and then he gets in his car and drives away.

'Where's Dad?' George asks when she comes downstairs.

'I have no idea,' I tell her.

Rachel's not here yet; she left to drive Martin home and then get changed, so George and I finish pouring the wine. 'I need your advice on something,' she says after we're done.

I follow her into the reading garden. We take a seat and she launches straight into the problem. 'I know you think I should go out with Martin. I know you like him.'

'I think you like him,' I say. 'And I know he likes you.'

'We talk a lot, it's true. I went to his house last night and met his mums and his little sister, and his dog.'

She talks some more about him, about the things they've been doing together. They went to see the new Tarantino film. They went to see *Aliens* at the cinema on Meko Street that shows older films. 'But there's this other boy. We write to each other in the Letter Library – or we did. And I know you'll say he's not here and Martin is, but I've liked him for a long time.' She takes a little breath. 'It's Cal.'

'Cal?'

'Cal Sweetie. Rachel's brother.'

She adds the bit about Rachel because I'm not saying anything and she assumes, I guess, that I'm not putting two and two together. I put them together the second she says his name, though; I'm just buying myself some time.

'He's been away for three years,' I say. 'How would he have gotten the letters in the book?'

'Tim Hooper,' she says. 'He delivered Cal's letters and took mine away.'

'And you don't think it could be Tim?'

'It's *Cal*,' she says forcefully. 'It's him. He's in France with his Dad. I want you to ask Rachel for his address so I can write to him there. I want to send him this letter.' She takes out a sealed envelope. 'If, for some reason, she doesn't want to give me the address, she could mail it herself.'

I take the envelope and put it in my pocket. 'Can I ask what it says?'

'It says I love him.'

It's such a huge thing for George to write. She doesn't make a joke and say we're shit at love. She's taking the first real chance of her life, and the really terrible thing is that she and Cal would have been perfect for each other. I hold the letter. And I try not to cry.

It'd be fair to say I feel slightly unhinged as I walk back from the reading garden into the bookshop. Dad's driven away. I haven't seen Mum for a week. George is in love with a dead person, and I can't stop thinking about kissing my best friend. Also, the end of the world is approaching. I'm tempted to drink some wine, but I know how that turns out.

Rachel walks in the door and stands next to me at the wine and cheese table. 'What's wrong?'

'Nothing. Everything is completely fine. Actually, I might call Mum about the sale.'

'You shouldn't sell the store,' she says.

'You've always called it a store, ever since we were kids. It's a book*shop*. It's not like some other retail store. It might be the same in a whole lot of ways, but this bookshop is special. Books are special, Rachel. Books are important. Words are important,' I say.

'Words matter, in fact. They're not pointless, as you've suggested. If they were pointless, then they couldn't start revolutions and they wouldn't change history. If they were just words, we wouldn't write songs or listen to them. We wouldn't beg to be read to as kids. If they were just words, then stories wouldn't have been around since before we could write. We wouldn't have learned to write. If they were just words, people wouldn't fall in love because of them, feel bad because of them, ache because of them, and stop aching because of them. If they were just words, then Frederick would not search desperately for the Derek Walcott.'

I stop and take a breath, and Rachel hands me a glass of water.

'I agree,' she says while I'm drinking. 'If you really feel that way, you should call your mum and stop the sale.'

I walk out the front of the bookshop and I feel completely unhinged now. Words do matter and they do start revolutions, but you can't eat a revolution. You can't pay the rent with a revolution. I'm walking up and down the street thinking about this when I turn around and see Amy standing there as if she's just materialized.

She stares at me for a while, and I stare back at her, and eventually she says, 'I'm sorry about Greg and the YouTube clip.'

'You took your time apologizing.'

'I wanted to come sooner, but Greg and I were breaking up.'

The minute she says it, I forget what I was out here for. She looks through the shop window, and back at me. She motions for me to follow her down the street. I stay where I am for all of five seconds and then I walk, as if I'm under some kind of spell.

'I can't do this anymore, Amy. I can't have you leave and come back, leave and come back.'

'So I won't leave anymore,' she says. 'I'm sure this time.'

Everyone's arriving for the book club. They say hello to me on the way past and I say hello to them, trying to look normal when I'm feeling anything but. After a group of people has walked inside, Amy and I are on the street alone again. The book club has started and I should go back inside, but I don't want to go.

Amy moves closer. 'Do you still have the ticket?' she asks, and I see us on the plane. I see us in New York at art galleries and shows and bookshops. I don't hesitate. I kiss her with the confidence that Rachel gave me, remembering her words. I am a great kisser. I'm a better kisser than Greg Idiot Smith.

The kissing goes on for a long time. Then there's laughing and talking and some kissing again and then more talking. Time passes and I don't feel it. Amy's back. She's mine again.

. . .

I walk into the shop, slightly dazed. Rachel's too focused on the book club to ask if I've called Mum, which is good. I can't tell her I didn't call because then I'd have to tell her why I didn't. I don't want to admit that in under an hour, Amy changed my mind about not selling the bookshop. There will be a time to tell Rachel, but that time isn't now.

I force myself to concentrate on the book club. Josie, who's been coming for about eight years, holds up a copy of *Where Things Come Back*, and I realize she's going to talk about her son dying. I start to warn Rachel, but she puts her fingers to her lips to make me quiet. When I'm not, she covers my mouth. I cover her ears without thinking. 'What are you doing?' she whispers.

'It's about death,' I whisper back.

'It's OK, Henry,' she says, and pulls my hands away from her ears. I pull hers from my mouth. We're close up, eye to eye, nose to nose, holding hands. 'I want to hear,' she says, and turns to the front, without dropping my hand. Josie starts off a round of people talking about their lives, sometimes connected to the books they've brought with them and sometimes not. Every one of them is talking about death.

'I'm OK,' Rachel says, because I'm staring at her, waiting for signs that she's not. When I look back, Frederick is standing in that formal way he has.

'My wife, Elena, died twenty years ago,' he says, and the room is so quiet. He tells the group about the night she died, when he sat next to her and read from her favorite book.

Rachel looks over at me. 'The Walcott,' we say together.

Rachel

I am a strange mix of things tonight. I am spark from Henry's hands and the memory of his kiss. I am warmth, blush from his stare, and calm, because I'm almost certain that he's mine and I'm his. He walked inside, and took my hand and held it in a way that let me know. It seems impossible at the same time that it seems like the thing that I knew was always going to happen.

I'm all these good things, and aching, too, and sad, because Josie is talking about her son. 'He was seven,' she says. 'Riding his bike. I was cheering him on. Then a car came round the corner and went up onto the sidewalk. Just collected him right up,' she says, and looks shocked, as if all the years haven't dulled that moment. She's staring at a spot of air in front of her, and I know, in that spot of air, is her son. At this moment, he might be lying on the sidewalk, as she saw him that day. But I'm certain that at other times, he's in that spot, grinning at her.

I'm crying, I realize, but I don't care.

Frieda talks about her brother, who died in a plane crash. Another woman called Marwa talks about her cousin who had cancer. Almost everyone in the group's lost someone.

Frederick is the last person to speak. Just before the book club ends, he says, 'My wife, Elena, died twenty years ago, almost to the day. I still miss her.' He tells the group about a book that Elena read to him from on their wedding night, and how he read to her from that same book, in the hospital, on the night that she died.

'The Walcott,' Henry and I say at the same time.

The book club ends not long after Frederick has spoken, but everyone mills around for a while, talking informally and eating the cheese. I like the feeling of the book club. It was more than a conversation about books. It was a conversation about people. I wish Mum could have been here to listen.

I help Henry clean up, and put the chairs away, all the while waiting until I see Frederick standing on his own. When there's a chance, I walk over and tell him that my brother, Cal, died. I wanted to say something to the whole group but I held back. It's really Frederick I want to tell, because I've known him a long time.

'I'm so very sorry,' he says.

'I can't swim anymore. I don't go in the ocean.'

As I say it, I wonder if it's true. I wonder if I'm speaking in the present tense, when really I should be speaking in the past. I wonder what I'd feel now, if I were there, looking at the water. It feels like both tenses are true – past and present. I love and hate the ocean. I want to be near it and I want to be away.

. . .

I can't stop thinking about the Walcott and Frederick and all the other people in the book club. I feel strangely calm and strong because of their tears. Henry's more determined than ever to find the Walcott after hearing the reason Frederick wants it. I'm determined too.

'We could look,' I say. 'When we go hunting on the fourteenth.'

'We won't find it by chance,' Henry says, and we sit close at the laptop, searching for a seller. There's only one copy, apart from an expensive edition, which we know won't be it. We're looking for an ordinary copy, which is anything but ordinary.

Henry sends the seller our information by email and while we wait for his reply, we lay out a bed of quilts and lie together.

'Why would Frederick give the book away?' Henry asks.

'Things get lost,' I say. 'Or maybe you can't stand to look at them.'

We lie quietly for a while, and then we hear the sound of an email coming in. Henry checks, and it's the seller saying we can visit on the fourteenth in the afternoon. 'It's down the coast,' Henry says after he looks up the address. He gives me a worried look.

'It's OK,' I tell him, and I think it might be. 'I have to see the ocean again sometime.' And at least I won't be alone.

Henry nods and tells me there's a story that his dad wants him to read and asks if he can read it aloud.

He gets the book from his bag, comes back, and lies next to me again. He holds it over our heads as he reads. The words could rain on us, I think. I have a strange image of us drinking them. Henry has changed me. He's changed the way I cry about Cal. The way I see the world.

The story is called 'Shakespeare's Memory', and it's about a German Shakespearean scholar who has been offered the memory of Shakespeare, from his boyhood to 1616. *It was as though I had been offered the ocean,* the narrator says.

But he doesn't understand that memory is abstract and chaotic. Memory isn't straightforward. It surfaces in sounds and images and feelings. He doesn't realize that in getting another person's memory, he will lose parts of himself.

After Henry has finished reading, he closes the book and goes quiet.

'What is it?' I ask.

'Nothing,' he says, and because I know Henry, I know it's something, but I don't push it. He says he needs to sleep, but I watch him stare at the ceiling. Every now and then he turns his head to the side and looks around the bookshop.

When Henry is finally sleeping, I leave the bookstore. I take the box out of the trunk before I drive away. I put it on the seat next to me. If I'm my memory, then Cal is his too, and I can't throw that box away. I can't look at it tonight, but I like the feel of it being next to me.

I keep my eyes ahead, but I have this strange feeling if I looked across, Cal might actually be here. I tell him that he was right and I've forgiven Henry. I tell him about Mum and how his death has changed us forever. That's the way it should be, I think. A death should change us forever. No two deaths should be the same.

I find myself in front of Lola's house. I text her because it's so late, and she texts back to say she's in the garage. I walk quietly through the garden toward the door. She's on the couch, legs folded beneath her.

'Have you finished recording the last song?' I ask.

'The plan was to record the last song at our last gig on Valentine's Day.'

'Fitting.'

'Only, Hiroko hasn't forgiven me. In her defense, I haven't said sorry.' She gives a sad grin. 'Every time I start to text her, I think that maybe she's considering staying. I think, if I keep my mouth shut, then maybe I'll get what I want.'

She turns the phone around and around in her hand. 'I know she can't stay.'

I lean my head on her shoulder.

'I don't know you as well as Henry,' she says. 'But I know something hasn't been right. You don't tell me a thing about what happened with Joel. You haven't been to the pool once since you arrived. I'm not stupid. I've noticed. I'm just waiting.'

I look at Lola's posters of all the bands that she loves – the Waifs, Warpaint, Karen O, Magic Dirt. I remember how Henry and I sat here in the afternoon on the couch while Lola played her songs for us.

Lola touches me with her toe, a gentle reminder that she's here. I tell her about Cal. The words still hurt, but they hurt less than they did when I told Henry, and maybe telling the next person will hurt even less.

'I was trying to imagine the worst thing,' Lola says. 'What's the worst thing that could have happened to you? Hiroko and I sat here trying to guess, so I could help you. We didn't guess that,' she says, and moves in close to me, and puts both arms around me, and we fall asleep like that.

The Broken Shore
by Peter Temple

Letters left between pp. 8 and 9
February 14, 2016

Dear George,

I was talking to Henry today, and he told me that it's the end of the world. Did you hear? I know how much you love Ray Bradbury, so I wondered if you'd like to spend the last night with me? We'd ignore the fact that it's Valentine's Day. We'd be strictly friends keeping each other company while we waited for the end to come. What do you think?

Martin

Dear Martin,

I'd like that a lot.

George

Henry

The last day of the world dawns bright and sunny, but a bad feeling follows me into the shower that I can't soap off or steam away. Yesterday I kept waiting for Amy to walk into the shop, and I was relieved when she texted around midday to let me know she wouldn't see me till Valentine's Day, when she hoped we'd meet at Laundry. Actually, I texted back, I promised Rachel a do-over. We're having another last night of the world, so I'll see you on the 15th.

Have you told her? Amy texts back.

About?

About us!

No chance yet, too busy, But I will.

I looked across the shop at Rachel, working in the Letter Library. I thought of George, and how Cal had missed out on her. I thought of how much Rachel wants us to have a last night, and decided I'd tell her about Amy and me after the world has ended.

I get out of the shower, dry myself off, and get dressed.

George knocks and walks in while I'm finishing up. 'Happy Valentine's Day,' she says, and reaches for her toothbrush.

'What happened to your reliable pessimism?' I ask.

'I have a friend to be with at school for the first time in six years. I no longer care what Stacy thinks. I have someone to spend the last night of the world with. I almost have a boyfriend. Did you give my letter to Rachel?'

'Yes.' No. 'Shit.'

'Shit?'

'I didn't mean to say that out loud. Everything is going to be fine.'

'Henry, everything *is* going to be fine. You told Mum not to sell,' she says, and kisses me, leaving peppermint lips on my cheek. 'Frieda told me. Rachel told her last night. She said you'd stepped out of book club to call Mum and tell her not to sell.'

Before I can set her straight, there's a knock on the bathroom door and it's Martin. 'Sorry. Your dad sent me up here to get George. He has to leave the store and he needs you to take over at the counter.'

'I'll be there in a minute,' George says, and turns to me. 'What's wrong, Hen?'

She hasn't called me Hen since we were kids.

'You really don't want to sell the bookshop? You don't care about the money?'

'I couldn't care less about money,' she says.

I can change my vote and fix things with the shop, but I can't save her from the hurt that'll come when she finds out about Cal. I want to tell her now to spare her some of that hurt, but I know that this is something that has to come from Rachel. 'Nothing,' I tell her. 'I'm glad you're happy.'

She leaves the bathroom, and after she's gone I sit on the edge of the bath and call Mum. I get her voicemail, so I leave a very definite message. 'Do not sell. I repeat: do not sell.'

Rachel's standing outside the door when I park the van in front of the warehouse. She's wearing a dress, and I find myself wondering if she's got a swimsuit on underneath it. It's brave of her to come with me to the beach, and it'd be even braver of her to swim. But Rachel is brave. Please don't disappear, I'm thinking, as she opens the van door and steps in.

The Lucksmiths are playing on the radio as we pull out of her street. I need to tell Rachel that Cal is George's mystery guy, but I decide not to tell her yet. I decide to let the both of us enjoy the day. Rachel looks happy. I'm happy with her.

'You're OK about where we're going?' I ask.

'Stop worrying, Henry. It's going to be fine. Or it won't be but I'll still be OK.'

I look over at her for a second. She's a hybrid now. The old Rachel and the new Rachel and possibly some other Rachels from the future are all tucked into her skin.

She rolls down the window and the day pours in – sunshine and dust. I turn up the music so it fills the car. 'Thank you,' she says. 'I don't feel unhappy.'

'I'm glad I could inspire such emotion.'

We reach the outskirts of the city. The concrete drops away and the trees start up and the sky gets bigger, stretched to pale blue. The road vibrates softly through the window and hums Rachel to sleep.

When she wakes, we're in a small town. She looks around and

smiles, smelling the loose blue air of the ocean. She wraps her arms around herself and follows me into a secondhand shop.

The entire back wall is full of books. I walk toward them and start looking through. Now that we're here, I can't help thinking that all I've done is drive her to the thing she now hates and show her a heap of books, which she sees every day at work.

But when I look at her she's kneeling on the floor, browsing through the nonfiction books. She's pulling them out, checking the titles. She stands after a while and walks over to the fiction section, where I am. I take out books, showing her the titles I love, and she takes them and reads the back of each. She flicks through, looking for notes in the margins.

'You're a Letter Library convert,' I say.

'I think I am,' she says. 'I love it. I'm glad you decided not to sell. The store is *you*, Henry.'

She says *you* in a way that Amy never has. She says my name in a way that Amy never does. She says it in the same way she says *love*, I realize. I notice a blue bathing strap showing near the neck of her dress, and I touch it without thinking.

'I might,' she says. 'It's the end of the world, after all. Would you swim with me?'

'I'm unprepared,' I say.

'I've seen you in your underwear,' she says.

'You've seen me naked,' I say.

She stares in my eyes, right in them, and I feel as though I might fall over.

'You have very large eyes,' I tell her.

'All the better to blink at you,' she says.

We're standing very close, and the conversation feels very sexy. I am wishing that I hadn't kissed Amy because if I hadn't, I think I would ask Rachel if she would kiss me again right now. I know she told me that our other kiss was to make Amy jealous, but I don't believe this anymore. I don't know why I believed it then. Because I know Rachel. As much as she's changed, I still *know* her. And if she didn't want to kiss me, she would never have kissed me.

'What?' she asks.

'What what?' I ask.

'You're smiling.'

'I just worked out something.'

'About?' she asks, and before I can say you, or us, or me, she points.

'You're holding a Walcott,' she says.

I hadn't even realized it was in my hands.

There are no markings on the book. There's no inscription. But I have this feeling it's the one. So does Rachel. We decide to take a chance, and skip going to the seller so we can have lunch.

We order and then stare at the Walcott that we've put in the middle of the table. 'I feel like it's a sign,' I say.

'I do too,' Rachel says, but neither of us says what we think it's a sign of. We keep smiling at each other and smiling at the book, and I keep thinking that I do really want to kiss Rachel and I want to kiss her for real.

'I think we should ask each other questions we always wanted to ask,' I say to her while we're eating.

'About?' she asks.

'About each other.'

'I know everything about you,' she says.

'Impossible. There are always more things to be known. I'll

prove it. I will ask questions of myself, and you will answer them, and we'll see if you get them right.'

'And shall we call the game Narcissism?'

'We shall call the game Henry. Question one: Who was my first kiss?'

'Amy,' she says.

'Incorrect.'

'Who?'

'You. I kissed you on the mouth in Year 4.'

'Really?'

'Kiss chasey. You don't remember?'

'I have no recollection,' I say. 'But trauma will do that to a person.'

'Question two: What is my favorite color?'

'Red. The color of Amy's hair.'

'Incorrect. It was red, and now it's blue,' I say, looking at her eyes. I'm looking for a sign that there's more between us than friendship, and I think maybe I see it in her face.

'So,' she says. 'Ask me another question.'

'No,' I say. 'Now we'll play the game of Rachel.'

She looks out of the window, in the direction of the ocean, and says the game of Rachel really needs to be played on the beach.

Rachel

I keep telling myself that there's some other way to interpret the game Henry's playing with me, some other way to interpret the way he looked at me in the bookstore before lunch. I keep telling myself that he kissed Amy and it's her that he loves. But my eyes are blue. He says I was his first kiss. He's here, flirting with me on the last night of the world. Amy is miles away.

'Now we'll play the game of Rachel,' Henry says, and before I think too much about it, I tell him the game of Rachel really needs to be played on the beach.

We're on the peninsula, less than two hours out of the city, the opposite direction from Sea Ridge. The ocean will look different and smell different. It will be called by a different name. But it will be the same unpredictable thing.

'Are you sure you want to go?' Henry asks, and I'm sure and not sure.

I've been thinking about it since the email from the seller came in and I knew we were going to the beach. I borrowed Rose's swimsuit this morning. It isn't exactly the best fit, but when I looked in the mirror, I felt right. Scared, and excited, too. I slipped my dress on over the top and told myself I didn't have to swim if I didn't want to. At least I'd be ready.

I've been away from the ocean too long, I think as we walk toward it. I thought about it in the bookstore as I watched Henry run his hands across the spines of books, hovering over the ones he particularly loved. I thought about him living a life without the bookstore, and at the same time I thought about me, living a life without the ocean. A dry, bookless world. It's too bleak even to imagine.

I can hear the water as we get closer, the hush of it, circling and flattening out. When it appears, I'm ready for it. It's long and achingly flat. Not the waves that heap over themselves continually back home.

Henry and I sit on the beach and stare at the water for a long time. This is the water of my dreams and nightmares. Sometimes it's the thing that takes Cal away, dragging him out on currents, and sometimes it's the thing that brings him back, bleached like that beaked whale, or sometimes, if I'm lucky, he's alive, and it spills him laughing onto the sand.

I tell Henry about the three layers of the ocean: the sunlight layer, the twilight zone, and the midnight zone, each named for the amount of sun in them. In the midnight zone, creatures have to make their own light. Before Cal died, the midnight zone was my favorite. The idea of no light fascinated me.

'I wanted to dive there, do you remember?' I ask, and he says he couldn't believe I could be that brave.

Bravery had nothing to do with it. I hadn't imagined that

anything terrible would ever happen. To me, or to the people I loved. I assumed the people I loved would always be safe. The ocean will always remind me that they won't.

I think about the things I wanted to see – killer whales and hatchet fish and vampire squid. I pored over books: dragonfish, metal and frill, teeth and eye; beautiful creatures, too, in colors that I've never seen in the surface world, both electric and pale, creatures glowing like fresh snow in the darkness. I wanted to see them with my own eyes.

'It scares me, but I want it again,' I tell Henry.

'You shouldn't feel guilty about that,' he says, and I wonder if that's what I've been waiting to hear. That I'm allowed to love it again.

'You want to swim?' he asks.

I'm not ready yet, though.

We sit for another hour. I watch the ocean, and Henry. He makes a sand castle and puts a ring of shells around the battlements. Before we leave, he walks to the edge to wash his hands. I think he does it deliberately, so he can come back and splash me, and I can feel the water on my skin.

There's a soft pink glow in the sky by the time Henry pulls up to Rose's so I can get ready for tonight. I remember something that Gus said to me once in one of our sessions. 'It'll just arrive. A feeling of being OK. If you do all the things we've talked about, it'll arrive.' He spoke as though it was a physical thing, something as real as a package that would come to me in the mail.

'Rachel,' Henry says. His face and the game he played earlier give me hope. 'It's – I mean . . .' He stops. I will him to keep going but he doesn't. 'It's nothing. I'll see you at the bookshop at seven.'

When I step out of the van, I catch a glimpse of myself in the window. I'm not the old me that I've been for the last ten months. I'm another me. I still don't quite recognize her. She looks, if I had to describe her, expectant.

By the time I get to the bookstore, the sky has clouded over. 'It'll rain by the end of the night,' I tell Henry when I'm inside.

'Let's hope not,' he says, and smiles nervously.

I smile nervously back.

We walk to Shanghai Dumplings, where his parents and Lola are meeting us. George and Martin are ahead of us on the street, and every time they get out of hearing distance, Henry starts to say something but then changes his mind. I know that he's going with Amy overseas. I know that. But part of me is desperate to believe that he's changed his mind and he wants me, and I can't get that hope to be quiet.

Mai Li gives us some menus after we've walked into the restaurant and tells Henry that his parents are fighting again. 'I don't know what about, but it seems pretty bad. Your mum's crying.'

We walk up the stairs, and we see that Mai Li's right. Sophia's eyes are red and there's a small smudge of mascara under her right eye. I take hold of Henry's hand, because I know how it is to see your mum like that.

We take our seats, and Lola arrives soon after us, and then there's an awkward silence because obviously we've all shown up and interrupted their fight, but Michael and Sophia are trying to act like nothing's wrong.

'What's going on?' Henry asks.

'Nothing,' Sophia says. 'We can talk about it later.'

'Your mother's sold the business,' Michael says.

'We all decided to sell the business,' Sophia says. 'We sat here and voted. And then you called me and told me to go ahead and look for buyers.'

'For the *business*,' Michael says, and from the way he says the last word, I know that Mum is right, that they're knocking down the place for flats. Michael confirms it. 'Developers are buying the place to demolish it, but don't worry, it's for an absolute fortune. We're rich,' he says, and then looks embarrassed by his sharp tone.

'I'm sorry,' he says, looking at me and Lola and Martin. 'This is very rude of us. We should discuss this later.'

'Undo it,' George says, speaking to Sophia. 'Tell them the deal's off.'

'She can't,' Michael says quietly, his voice under control now. 'It's done. It's gone.'

'It can't be gone. It's our home,' George says.

'You should have spoken up before,' Sophia says gently.

'I'm speaking up now,' George says. 'And maybe I would have spoken up before if you hadn't made me feel like I was in the middle of something. Henry took back his vote.'

'Henry took it back this morning, which was too late,' she says.

Henry doesn't say anything. He looks shocked and ashamed. I take his hand again and hold it.

'What's everyone reading?' Sophia asks, but no one answers her.

'I read *Cloud Atlas*,' I say eventually. 'Henry's read it too.'

'I've read it,' George says halfheartedly. 'It's a *fucking* good book.'

'I'm with George,' Sophia says. 'Worthy of the *F* word, yes. Good book. The characters all share the same birthmark, don't they? Are they all the same person?'

'Not the same person,' Henry says, still looking at his plate. 'They've got the same soul.'

'It's about the transmigration of the soul,' I say. 'At least, I think. About the possibility that a soul can move on to another body after death.'

'Does anyone believe in that?' Martin asks. 'That souls can transmigrate?'

'I do,' says George.

'I don't,' I say. 'I don't believe in reincarnation, either.'

'What do you believe in?' Sophia asks.

For all my thinking about this, I haven't changed my view. But I've changed what I *want* my view to be. I love the idea that Cal's soul could find a way to transmigrate. The moment on the beach when I realized that he was gone would have been so much easier if I'd known that the center of Cal, the thing that made him Cal, had traveled somewhere, disappeared, but not gone, turning into something else – even turning into clouds would have been better than ash.

'*Transmigrate* comes from the Latin *transmigrare*.' Michael finally speaks. 'Meaning "moved from one place to another". So it's not necessarily the movement of the soul. *Trans* means "across" or "beyond".'

'Or "through",' Henry says. '"On the other side of".'

Everyone keeps on the subject of books, since it's safe. Lola says she read *Fifty Shades of Grey* and Henry covers his ears. George says she wants to read it and her dad covers his ears. Martin says he read a Peter Temple that George suggested, and the talk turns to literary crime. There's a small truce drawn, but I'm only partly listening.

I'm thinking of the transmigration of memory. Not the transmigration that happened in the Borges story, but the transmigration of memory that happens all the time – saving people the only way we can – holding the dead here with their stories, with their marks on the page, with their histories. It's a very beautiful idea, and, I decide, entirely possible.

Henry

I can't believe I gave the bookshop away because I thought I should be like Greg Smith. I look into my future tonight, stare down the road of it, and I'm walking past an ugly high-rise, flats, and I'm telling my kids that there, right there, was the most beautiful building, the building where I grew up.

'Where is it now?' they'll ask, and I'll tell them I threw it away on a girl who didn't love me to compete with a guy I knew all along was a total idiot. In short, kids, your father really fucked up.

I can't look at Dad tonight. I'm too ashamed. I'm too sad. I study the tablecloth, every inch of the pattern. I concentrate on the circles. I trace them with my eyes, finding the end of one, and following it around to the start of another. It's the same tablecloth that's always been here. Every table has one. I've never noticed all the little circles before.

Rachel holds my hand, which is the only good thing about the dinner. I could get through quite a bit in life with her holding my hand. She's my best friend, whether I'm broke or not. She's my best friend despite having seen me drool on pillows. She's dragged me out of the girls' toilets; she wants to spend the last night of the world with me.

I look at the big picture. I want to be with Rachel, but it's not a choice between her and Amy. I'm not sure I can have her, for a start. But even if I could, the choice is about the kind of person I want to be with. I choose to be with a person who's acting like my best friend. I might not be lucky enough for that person to be Rachel, but it definitely isn't Amy, the girl who comes and goes. The girl who, if I'm honest, has always been a little bit in love with someone else while she's with me.

The conversation turns from transmigration to *Fifty Shades of Grey*. I go to the bathroom to work out the speech I want to give, the words I want to say to our family to hold us together in the face of losing the bookshop. When I come back all set to give it, everyone's getting ready to go.

'I'm going home,' George says to Mum, and leaves with Martin. Dad walks in the opposite direction. I'm not sure where he's going, and he doesn't look entirely sure either. Mum offers me and Rachel and Lola a lift to Lola's last gig, but I won't take it. I kiss her on the cheek and tell her I'll call her later.

Rachel and Lola both hold my hands on the way to Laundry. There's nothing to say that'll make this better. 'How could I not know *how* bad it would feel to lose the bookshop? I've got a great imagination.'

There's a crowd out in front of Laundry. People from school are lining up to hear the Hollows' last show. 'They'll be disappointed,' Lola says. 'Since it's just me.'

'You haven't apologized?' I ask, not quite believing it.

'Not directly,' she says.

I look at Rachel and she looks at me, and I know that I've been delegated the spokesperson here. 'OK, Lola, it might be time for some truth telling. You and Hiroko are best friends.'

'More than that – you write together,' Rachel says.

'And sometimes you put music before pretty much everything else,' I tell her.

'You're obsessed with the Hollows,' Rachel says.

'And Hiroko is way more important than you being famous,' I finish.

'Wow,' Lola says. 'That's actually good advice coming from two people who've almost completely fucked up their friendship on more than one occasion.'

She takes out her phone and pauses for a second before calling. 'H?' Lola says, and mouths at us that it's her voicemail. 'I need you to come tonight. Not for the recording. I don't care about the recording. I want us to play one last song together. We don't have to play the whole gig – just one last song.' She goes quiet, and then she says, 'And I don't think you'd be nothing without me. I think the opposite. I need you, H.'

She hangs up and breathes out. 'Let's hope she checks her voicemail.'

As soon as Lola's walked off, I start thinking about the bookshop again.

'It will be OK,' Rachel keeps saying.

'How? How will it be OK? It is the end of the world. It is the actual end of the world.'

'It's not.'

'You're right. The end of the world would be better than this.'

'*Henry,*' she says, and out of nowhere. 'I love you.'

And it's a small spot of light in the darkness. It's brilliant, unbelievably brilliant. Life is still shit, but it's great at the same time.

Honesty and bravery are contagious, so I take Rachel's hands. I'm shaking a little, which is to be expected since I'm about to tell her that I love her, too.

'Rachel,' I say.

'Henry,' she says.

And then Amy appears beside us, takes my hand from Rachel's, and says, 'Thanks for keeping him warm. We got back together Friday night. Didn't you know?' She smiles, turns my face to hers, and kisses me.

I know, for certain, that when I'm old and I'm losing my memories, I will always feel the warmth of Rachel's hand leaving mine.

I blink, and Rachel's face has changed. She's smiling harder. It's fake, but only I would know it. 'That's great,' she says to Amy. 'Really great.' She points to the line that's moving. 'You should go inside. See Lola.'

'I don't want to go. I promised you an apocalypse and that's what you're getting.'

'I'm OK,' she says. 'We've spent a great day together and you should be with Amy, especially after losing the bookstore.'

I don't want to be with Amy. 'Wait. Please,' I say to Rachel, and I turn around to ask Amy to please give me a minute and some privacy, and then I say quietly to Rachel, 'Do you love me?'

She looks at me, her eyes serious. 'You'll always be my best friend. I love every single thing about you. I would not want to live without you. But I don't love you in the way you're asking me if I love you. What I meant before was, I love you as a friend.'

'I don't believe you,' I say.

'*Believe* me,' she says. 'I'm fine.'

'And the kiss?'

'Didn't mean anything,' she says. 'Really. You don't need to worry about me. Go. Be with Amy. I'm most likely going back to Joel.'

I don't believe she doesn't love me, but I do believe I've lost her. She's wearing the same face she wore when she first came back. A stranger's face. I can actually feel a chasm opening in my chest.

'I'll see you both in there,' she says, and walks ahead of Amy and me into the crowd.

I take a seat outside because I need air. I go talk to Amy. It's an understatement to say that this is turning into a really shit night.

'Henry, what's wrong?' Amy asks.

'We're selling the bookshop,' I tell her.

'I know,' she says, and smiles. 'You'll make a fortune from that place. I could never work out why you didn't sell it before.'

Because I love it. Because I love books in a way that's beyond logic and reason. That's just how it is. I love them the way those people in the Letter Library love them. It's not enough to read – I want to talk through the pages to get to the other side, to get to the person who read them before me. I want to spend my life hunting them, reading them, selling them. I want to serve customers and put the right book in their hands. I want to talk to Frederick and Frieda. I want to listen to the book club. I want it all. And I want it to go on forever. And if it can't, then I want it right up to the very last second. And I want a girl who wants me the same way. Dust and all.

'Why did you come back to me, Amy? Was it because you saw Rachel kiss me?'

'No.'

'It feels like it,' I say. 'It feels like I'm always plan B.'

My family might be shit at love, but I know what love's *not* when I see it. At least I do now. I feel like a bit of a dickhead thinking back on all the times I've thrown myself at Amy over the years. I'm not too hard on myself, though, because I think there's probably a lot of people in the world who've felt like a bit of a dickhead because they've thrown themselves at a person they love who doesn't love them back. So, statistically speaking, I'm average, and I can live with that.

'I've done a heap of things to prove I love you,' Amy says. She rambles on about the money she lent me for the trip, and the time she went to the dance with me, and the time she lent me her car. 'If you think you have a chance with Rachel, you don't. She doesn't love you, she just hates me.'

'Rachel's not like that.'

'She is. I've read the letter that proves it,' she says.

'What?' I ask, and now I'm remembering something from the night that Rachel saved me in the toilet. 'What letter?'

She doesn't answer.

'If you ever liked me at all, Amy, please tell me.'

'It was Year 9, on the last night of the world. We got back to your house and you took me upstairs to show me your room, and while you were in the bathroom, I flicked through the book on your bed. She'd left a note in there telling you to look in a book in the Letter Library. I can't remember the name anymore.'

'Was it the *Prufrock*?' I ask.

'That sounds like it,' she says. 'When we went downstairs, I took the letter. I wanted us to spend the last night together and I thought if you read it, you'd choose her and leave me.'

'And the letter said?' I ask, but I know what the letter said – I love you. 'Do you still have it?' I ask, and she says she put the letter into another book, one she didn't think I'd look in. 'Which one?'

'A book with a yellow cover,' she says, and I close my eyes in frustration. 'With a Japanese name that started with *K*.'

'Kazuo Ishiguro?'

'Maybe.'

Never Let Me Go? I ask.

'Possibly,' she says. 'Are you mad?'

I stare at the girl that I've loved for almost four years and tell her I'm not mad. I am a little bit, but she did it to be with me. And I realize tonight how much Amy hates being alone. Her idea of torture is an overseas holiday without a friend for company. But that friend can't be me.

I leave her behind and go inside. I have a girl to find. I have a bookshop to say good-bye to.

I pay my money and push my way through the crowd, looking for Rachel. I call for her over people's heads, not caring what I look or sound like. 'Rachel!' I'm yelling as I get to the front near the stage. 'Can you see her?' I yell to Lola. She scans the crowd and shakes her head.

I call her but get no answer. I leave a message telling her I'm coming to the warehouse. I'm about to leave when I look back at Lola. She's alone at the mike, waiting for Hiroko, who might not arrive, and I just can't leave her there alone.

She gives up waiting for Hiroko and starts to play. She's looking at me as she does, and I'm looking at her. The Hollows might have played their last song, but I'm still here and I'm her friend. I can't sing, but fuck it. I haul myself onto the stage with her anyway.

She stops what she's playing and starts an Art of Fighting song that she knows I know, and I sing the words with her. We finish that and start on some Ben Folds, because I know his albums too. We're almost through the fourth song when I hear the small ping of a triangle. I look over and Hiroko's standing in the background. 'I didn't have time to bring my glockenspiel,' she says.

I move to step off the stage, but Hiroko hands me the triangle and she takes over my mike. 'Thank God,' someone yells from the crowd.

'Shut up,' Lola says into the mike, and whoever the 'someone' is, he does.

'Shut up, everyone,' Lola continues. 'I've got something to say. This girl is the best lyricist I know. She's the best percussionist. And I'm going to miss her.'

Hiroko grins, and counts them down to the start of their last song.

I leave the two of them up there. I swing myself down from the stage and push myself through the crowd. It might not be the end of the world, but it feels like Rachel and I don't have any more time to lose.

Rachel

I leave Henry with Amy. I'm OK. I'm crying, but that's OK. So Henry's gone back to Amy? Henry was always going back to Amy. I knew that. I've just been kidding myself. I'm in love with him now, sure, but in the future, if I can just get there, someone else entirely is waiting for me.

I find a space at the back of Laundry where Henry won't see me. I watch with my breath held while Lola sings alone. Then I watch as Henry climbs onstage to sing with her. He's got many talents, but singing really isn't one of them. But he's spectacular. I hope Amy's good to him this time.

I watch until Hiroko walks out onstage and Lola announces that she's going to miss her and they start their last song. It's the first one she and Hiroko ever wrote. They sang it to Henry and me one day in her garage. I need the music to be louder so I don't keep hearing myself say I love you, hearing Amy thank me for keeping him warm.

I go into the bathroom to wash my face. Katia's in there. 'Did it work out with Shakespeare?' she asks, and I tell her he's going overseas with Amy.

'That's a shame. He missed out on you.'

I walk out of the club, across the road, and back into the bookstore. I could go home to the warehouse, but I want to be with the books. I want to continue cataloging the Letter Library. It's more important now than ever to record those notes on the pages. It's not that they'll be lost. They were written, so they'll always exist. But they'll be lost for Michael, and I hate that thought.

My plan is to keep cataloging all night to take my mind off Henry and Amy, who are probably kissing by now back at the bar. I open my computer and take out a stack of books. I begin flipping the pages of the first one, but I'm too restless tonight.

I take out *Sea* and look through it, searching again for a line from Cal that I've missed. There's a small mark on the page with the jellyfish, but it's not his writing. I know his as well as I know my own writing. He was always scribbling things. On that last day, a minute before he went into the water to take that last swim, he was writing. He was lying down, propped up on one arm, wearing Mum's floppy hat and Audrey Hepburn sunglasses. He was writing in one of the notebooks he always used, the ones with the perforated edges, so he could tear out the pages neatly.

I feel someone standing behind me, and I turn to see George. She's staring at *Sea,* and I tell her I was wondering if Cal had left a letter in the book at some stage or another. 'It's not important,' I lie.

'He did,' she says, and holds out the copy of *Pride and Prejudice and Zombies.*

I see Elizabeth on the cover, face half eaten away so her teeth and vocal cords are showing.

George hands me a letter. It's written on the kind of paper that Cal used, the kind of paper that he used that day. It feels soft and frail, which might be my imagining, or it might be that George has read it so many times. I'll catalog it later, I know. I'll catalog it more carefully than any of the other letters I've found in the Letter Library. Michael was right – it's a library of people.

Pride and Prejudice and Zombies

by Jane Austen and Seth Grahame-Smith

Letter left between pp. 44 and 45

November 25, 2013

> *Dear George,*
>
> *I understand your concern that I might be a psychopath. I'm not, but I also understand that all psychopaths probably say that. So, here's my sister to prove it:*
>
> *My brother is usually not a psychopath.*
>
> *She doesn't know why she's writing that. She's watching a documentary. She'd sign away her life if you asked her to while she's watching Brian Cox.*
>
> *I hope you keep writing to me,*
>
> *Pytheas*

It makes perfect sense, with hindsight – the Sea-Monkeys, the small note on *Sea* that I imagine was Cal pointing out the thing he loved to George.

'Pytheas was the first explorer to link the moon with the tides,' I say.

'I know,' George says. 'It is Cal, isn't it?'

I nod.

'I love him,' she says.

It makes me deliriously happy. It breaks my heart.

'Do you think he loves me?' George asks, and I nod.

She smiles. It's such a brilliant smile, full of hope, that I can't look at it.

'I gave Henry a letter from me to Cal to give to you. I need you to post it to him.'

I say that I'll be back in a minute, and I walk toward the bathroom. There's someone in there. I stand outside waiting, thinking about how unfair the world is – that Cal could have had George. She loved him and he loved her and if he hadn't gone for a swim that day, then they'd be together now.

It's Frederick who's in the bathroom. He comes out and notices that I'm upset. 'I might be intruding,' he says, in that polite, formal way he has. 'But are you all right?'

'No,' I tell him.

And standing here in the doorway of the bathroom, I tell him what just happened. I let it all out – how I've lied to George and now I have to break her heart and tell her that Cal is dead.

I don't expect Frederick to really understand. My words are a jumble and I'm crying while I speak. But he nods and listens, and then he tells me some more about his wife, Elena.

'We had a shop, this shop actually, when it was a florist's.'

With everything that's happened so far tonight, it's hard to take that in. 'You and she lived and worked *here*?' He nods, and I think about how he's come here every day since.

'I couldn't stand to be in here without her. Everything in it reminded me of her. It was unbearable. I didn't tell anyone about her. I lied to people so they wouldn't ask questions. I sold this place for nothing,' he says. 'I didn't care. I wanted to burn it. I tried one night, but Elena stopped me.'

'You saw her?' I ask. 'You saw her ghost?'

He nods and looks right at me, his eyes completely serious. 'I am certain that she kept blowing out the match.'

I'm exhausted from crying, and I have to go back to George soon. But I stand here with Frederick. Because he's about to lose the florist shop for the second time, and I can imagine what that might feel like.

'I don't know how to tell her,' I say into the quiet.

'Perhaps start by telling her she was loved.'

This is where I start. We sit out in front of the bookstore so we can have some privacy.

'It is Cal,' I tell her again. 'It was him.' As gently as I can, I tell her that he died.

She stares up at a sky that actually looks starless tonight. It's not. A sky can't be starless. But the lights of the city are doing their best to drown them out.

'He died almost a year ago now.' I expect her to be angry, but she's completely still, except for the pressure she puts on my hand.

'What happened?' she asks, and I start anywhere. I don't know where the beginning is, really.

I describe him on the beach, in Mum's floppy hat and huge sunglasses, writing a letter.

'Mum and I were talking about the future. My future. We were planning what college I'd go to, talking about the best ones for marine biology.

'He put down his pen, took off his hat and glasses, and ran toward the water, calling for me to follow him, but I stayed on the beach talking with Mum.'

I can see Cal running into the water under this thin and yellow light while Mum and I sat on the beach and talked about tomorrow.

The thing that most people don't realize about drowning is that it's quiet. Cal was such a good swimmer, the possibility of him dying that way didn't occur to us. He and I had been much farther out on other days. We'd swum at night, in dangerous places, and we were fine. It makes no sense that he died that day, at that time, when the waters looked so still.

He drowned while I asked Mum if I could have a belly-button ring, and she said yes and asked me how they did it. He drowned while I waved away a fly. While I looked at the buckled trees, while I imagined sex with Joel, while I excavated sand with my toes.

'We tried to save him,' I say. 'We got him to the beach.'

I don't tell her about Mum standing quickly and looking into the water. How I started laughing, and said, 'What?' because I thought Cal was doing something funny.

'I can't see him,' she said, taking off her dress before she ran. These are the lost seconds that haunt Mum. 'Why did I bother taking off my *fucking* dress?' I've heard her say to Gran. 'Why?'

'Because you did,' Gran said. 'And it wouldn't have mattered. He was gone.'

I tell George instead that Cal died in the place he loved the most. I tell her it was quick, which I know, outside of nightmares, it would have been. I tell her that I think, although I can't know, that the last thing he did was write her a letter. He was writing something, and I hope it was to her.

I tell her how far he'd thought himself into the future, to when he would dive off the Gulf of Mexico, in the Green Canyon. I tell her about that canyon – about the animals he imagined seeing, far below the surface, where the sunlight can't reach. I tell her about the light down there, light from billions of microorganisms that glow in the dark. Spots of light – like drifting snow.

She and I walk to my car. I take the box out of the trunk and we sit on the curb to look through it. There are journals and comics and a small world globe that I gave Cal for Christmas once. Keys to his bike lock, some coins, his swimming goggles and a penknife. His library card, a CD. Maybe it seems strange to George that this is the box of things that Gran gave to me. But everything in here is important to me. It's his life. I know that, years in the future, I will still have these things. There will never be a time when I don't want them, all the tiny parts of Cal that made a life.

In the journal, just as I expected, there's a letter for George. I hand it over without looking at it, and she reads it aloud to me. Cal loved George and she loved him back, and that's no small thing. I look up at the light-drowned sky. I locate a star.

The letter is beautiful and brave, and hearing Cal's words makes me know for certain that Henry was right. I've had the world the wrong way around. It's life that's important. Cal knew that.

He was living right up until the last second, leaving that note for George. I have to tell Henry that I lied. I do love him.

Before I leave, I ask George if she'll be all right. 'Can I get Martin for you?'

'Actually, I'd like that,' she says. 'He's in the reading garden.'

I go inside and bring him back to her.

She doesn't say much to him, just that Cal is dead. She's crying as she says it. 'It's shit,' she says, wiping her eyes with her sleeve. 'Really shit. I need a friend.' Martin sits on the curb and puts his arm around her.

Letter undated

Dear George,

It's the start of March; the end of summer, but it's still warm. Not a lot of time left to swim.

I'm on the beach with my mum and my sister. My sister is Rachel Sweetie. I'm Cal Sweetie. Yep. The tall, skinny, goofy guy you've known pretty much all your life. Are you disappointed? I understand if you're disappointed. I really hope you're not disappointed.

I think we should at least go out on a date. One date. That way, you can see if you like me in person.

I'm about to go for a swim. And then I'm going to mail this letter to Howling Books. My friend Tim was putting the letters in the books for me, but he's moved away.

So if you want to write back, send the letter to 11 Marine Parade, Sea Ridge 9873.

Love, Cal

Henry

I think about going to the bookshop to get the letter, but I decide I can't wait that long and take a cab straight to the warehouse. I keep calling Rachel on the way, but I only get her voicemail. I call again and again but she doesn't pick up. I leave message after message. 'I messed up. I just didn't know what I know now. It's you and the bookshop that I want. I don't need loads of money. I can live without a definite future as long as you're in that indefinite future with me.'

I'm in what I'd describe as a love fever. I ask the cab driver if he can go any faster. He points out that we're not going at all, since we're stuck in a traffic jam. 'Someone's broken down up ahead,' he says.

'Of course they have,' I say, and put my head out of the window to see what's happening. There's something close to a four-car pileup, so we're going nowhere fast. I pay the fare and begin running. The rain starts that Rachel predicted earlier in the day.

It doesn't just start. It's one of those summer thunderstorms that really hammers the ground, and anyone in the way of the ground. The thunder joins in but I keep running, splashing up water as I go.

By the time I reach Rachel's place, I'm soaked. I bang on the door and yell Rachel's name. Her aunt opens the door and frowns. 'I know I fucked up,' I tell her, trying to speak through the heaving breaths I'm taking. 'But I can fix it if I can just talk to her.'

'She's not here,' she says. 'How did you fuck up?'

'She didn't say?'

'I haven't seen her.'

'Fuck,' I say, looking up at the rain and knowing I just spent my last bit of money on the taxi. *'Fuck.'* I look at her. 'I don't have any money.'

'Wait a minute,' she says. 'I'll drive you.'

I'm out of the car as soon as Rose stops, running into the bookshop, water dripping off me all over the floor. I scan the Letter Library, looking for *Never Let Me Go.* Nothing gets removed from the Library, so if Amy put the letter in the book three years ago, it should still be here today.

I hold the book for a minute or two, hoping. Then I flick through it and find a thin sheet of paper with Rachel's handwriting on it.

December 12, 2012

Dear Henry,
I'm leaving this letter on the same page as 'The Love Song of J. Alfred Prufrock' because you love the poem,

and I love you. I know you're out with Amy, but fuck it – she doesn't love you, Henry. She loves herself, quite a bit, in fact. And I love you. I love that you read. I love that you love secondhand books. I love pretty much everything about you, and I've known you for ten years, so that's saying something. I leave tomorrow. Please call me when you get this, no matter how late.

Rachel

I have this feeling as I hold it, that even though the bookshop is sold, all isn't lost. We lose things, but sometimes they come back. Life doesn't always happen in the order you want.

Dad walks in from the reading garden. I see through the back window there's a small party of sorts going on. Frederick, Frieda, and Frank are all drinking beer. 'Is the gate open between us and the bakery?' I ask.

'Frank opened it with a crowbar when he heard the news that we'd sold.'

'Too late,' I say.

'Better late than never,' Dad says.

'I'm sorry,' I tell him. 'I didn't realize they were planning on knocking the place down.'

'It wasn't your dream, Henry,' he says. 'It's not your fault.'

'But it was my dream,' I tell him.

He thinks about that, and eventually he says, 'Well, that's a hard lesson to learn. But you won't give away the next one.'

Dad tells me that Rachel is here somewhere; she was talking to George earlier about Cal. 'It's very sad,' he says, so I know that George has heard the news.

'He was writing in this Library,' Dad says. 'It'll be terrible to lose it. We can't possibly keep all of these books, which is why I wanted Rachel to catalog them. She's only half done. There won't be time to finish it now.'

'But why can't you keep it? Keep the whole thing?' I ask.

He waves up and down the shelves. 'It's huge, Henry, and I already have copies of all of these books.'

'We could house it,' I say. 'In the shed.'

'What shed?' he asks.

'The shed of wherever we all move together.'

He smiles at me, and waits for me to catch up.

'We're not all moving together?'

'I thought I might travel. See Shakespeare's country and some plays in the West End. Keep going from there to Argentina. Perhaps learn Spanish and read Borges without an interpreter before I die.'

'You're not dying.'

'Well, not immediately, Henry.'

'And George and me?'

'Well, George will go to live with your mother, I suppose. And you, Henry, you have that round-the-world ticket.'

Dad stands, puts his hand on my shoulder. 'I think perhaps your mother may be right, Henry. We make very little and none of us can live on dreams.'

'You need some dreams,' I say.

'Dreams and a little money,' he says, and then walks out to the garden, where the others are sitting and commiserating, celebrating the end.

When I turn around, Rachel is standing there. 'I was out in the front. You ran right past me.'

'I didn't see you.'

'Obviously,' she says.

I find myself mesmerized by her. I try to look like I'm not wondering what's underneath her clothes, but I am wondering and I'm wondering whether I'll be lucky enough to see it one day.

Focus, Henry. 'I think you do love me,' I say. 'I have proof.' I hold up the letter. 'It has your signature on it. A person might call it a contract.'

'There's a date on that letter. I don't think you can hold me to a love contract I signed three years ago in a state of sugar madness.'

'I don't think you can date a letter like this. A love letter, by definition, should be timeless or what's the point? I love you, but only for 2012 and then my love expires? What's the universe's problem with forever? It lets the geese get away with it.'

'The geese?' Rachel asks.

'They mate forever.'

'That's not strictly true,' she says, and then she interrupts herself, takes hold of my T-shirt, ignoring that I'm soaked, and pulls me close. 'That was a very nice speech, but it was all about me loving you, Henry.'

'Really? There was meant to be a bit that was the other way around. It was meant to be the first thing I said.'

'You left it out.'

'You are my best friend. You are the best person I know. You are spectacular, Rachel Sweetie,' I say. 'I love you.' And then I kiss her.

Later, much later, at a time that is unknown to me at this point, I will unbutton Rachel slowly. I will kiss her collarbone, and think of watermelon in summer, explored down to the rind. I will hope and imagine that I can see our lives from above the universe, hope that we are together for the course of our lives.

But at this moment, it is a kiss. It is a kiss that continues while we put the 'Prufrock' letter back in the book and back in the Library. It is a kiss that continues while I lead her up the stairs for some privacy. It is a kiss that continues through the years.

But at this moment, it is just the start.

After we have been in my bed a while, Rachel leans over to check her voicemail.

'I left some messages.'

'So it seems.'

'I felt it was important that you understand the situation.'

'Which is?'

'I'm very fond of you.'

She asks me if I gave Frederick the Walcott we found today. I haven't yet, so we go down to the reading garden. It's very late but everyone is still up. Mum is there now, along with Dad; Frank, Frieda and Frederick are all there. Rachel and I take our seats and I hand the Walcott to Frederick.

From the way that he holds it, I'm almost certain it's not Elena's copy. 'Bookshop or no bookshop, I'll keep looking,' I tell him.

'Thank you, Henry,' he says, and when he tries to give me money for this copy, Rachel and I both insist it's on the house.

We all sit here missing the bookshop before it's gone, working out the logistics of what to do with the stock. Mum's crying as much as any of us, and I know this is just as hard for her.

I catch her looking at me. 'You've grown up,' she says when I ask her what she's thinking. 'I hadn't noticed.'

Rachel

Henry was in the middle of a rant when I pulled him close and kissed him. He was waving my letter and querying the validity of love that's date-stamped. I had a whole speech planned. I was going to make him explain, point by point, why it was me he loved and not Amy, before I admitted that I loved him too. I was going to ask for proof.

But then I decided that proof was overrated, and maybe not even possible and would very likely spoil the moment – a moment that I've been waiting for, for a long, long time.

So I decided to take control of the situation and kiss him. It felt as though we were trapped in honey. And the rest of what we did, and how we did it, and the words that were said, are secret.

Lying in Henry's bed later, life feels different from how it was before. There are things other than death, I know that now. Henry and I move in and out of sleep, talking and being quiet. His window is open and the warm night drifts through. I put my feet on the window ledge to feel it. Thoughts pass between us. We are the books we read and the things we love. Cal is the ocean and the letters he left. Our ghosts hide in the things we leave behind.

Henry and I go downstairs after a while, to give the Walcott to Frederick. It isn't the one that he's looking for. It's out there, Henry tells him, and he promises to keep looking.

Frederick leaves before the rest of us, and when I walk back inside, I see that he's put the Walcott on the shelf of the Letter Library. It's facing out. There's a letter in it, and it's for me. I know it before I open the book.

> *Dear Rachel,*
>
> *I hope you don't mind that I'm writing to you. But I have been thinking about our conversations, and the great sadness that you must be feeling.*
>
> *I lost my wife twenty years ago, and sometimes I feel as if I have lived without her for a decade, and sometimes I feel as though I lost her just a minute before.*
>
> *I write 'lost', but I have grown to hate that expression. She was not a set of keys or a hat. The equivalent is saying that I have misplaced my lungs.*
>
> *I know you understand what I mean. I can see it in your face. There comes a time when the nongrievers go back to life, even some of the grievers, and you're left trying to comprehend the incomprehensible.*
>
> *What's the point in living on past the moment when those we have loved have left us? And how can we ever*

forgive ourselves for letting them go? I thought about these things a great deal after my wife died. I met her when I was twenty-one. She was my best friend. I could not imagine life without her. Without her in the world, time did not exist. A world without time is a terrible thing. There is no certainty. Days could move quickly or slowly, or not at all. The laws of the universe have been tinkered with, and you are blindly wheeling. There is no grip in a world like this. And a kind of madness takes over.

But you know this already, Rachel.

You know that you must hold on to any laws that you can find.

I love my son, and he is the law that cannot be tinkered with. Love of the things that make you happy is steady too – books, words, music, art – these are lights that reappear in a broken universe.

Do people have a choice in the direction their lives will go? We cannot choose where and when we are born, by whom or how we are first loved, or with whom we will fall in love – at least, I do not believe so. And we cannot choose who is taken from us, or the way in which they are taken.

I tried to save my wife. I tried to resuscitate her while I waited for the ambulance. I think often about that last kiss – breathless in a way so different from the first. And I comfort myself with the thought that I tried. And that it was beyond my control.

But I do believe we have choices – how we love and

how much, what we read, where we travel. How we live
after the person we love has died or left us. Whether or
not we decide to take the risk and live again.

But what is the point? I imagine you asking. For
me it is this. On a night when I could hear the ocean
coming in through the window of my room, a woman
I would marry and have a child with told me she loved
me. Our son was just a hint on our skins. The stars were
milk on the darkness. I did not think about losing her.
I thought only that she loved me, and we were happy.

You say that the ocean is the most beautiful thing
you've ever seen, and the thing that terrifies you the
most. This describes how it was for me to fall in love
with Elena. Perhaps all things that are worthwhile are
terrifying?

I sold our florist shop as soon as she died, but I
couldn't stay away. Go back to the ocean, Rachel. It's a
part of you, and so is Cal.

Frederick

In the morning, while Henry is still sleeping, I go downstairs to sit
in the garden. There are people sitting there already, even though
the bookstore isn't open. They've come through from Frank's,
bringing their croissants and coffee. They ask me what time the
bookstore opens, and I tell them the hours – ten till it depends,
really.

I try not to think about the time when the reading garden will
be gone. I try to look on the practical side. People need housing. I

can't make myself believe that it's a good thing they have it here, though.

Frank gives me my coffee. 'On the house. It's a day of national mourning.'

I hear a soft cough, and I turn to see Frederick. 'Thank you for the letter,' I say, and we eat breakfast together. I think about Frederick owning the bookstore when it was a florist shop. I think about *Cloud Atlas*, and how, in the novel, all the separate stories, in the end, added up to one.

I tell Frederick that, yes, I'll do Year 12 again eventually, but I think first I'll ask Rose to fund me a round-the-world ticket – a loan, not a gift – so I can go with Henry. Before anything I'll go home to Sea Ridge.

I'll show Mum the catalog of the Letter Library. I'll tell her about the people who have loved and lost and left a record of it. I'll tell her to prove we're not alone, and that all the different stories that there are somehow all add up to one. I'll tell her about Cal and George. I'll tell her about the idea that memory can transmigrate, from the dead to the living. I'll tell her about the beautiful, impossible thought that Cal might have, at the moment of dying, transmigrated. I'll tell her that I think he had been transmigrating all his life: leaving himself in the things he loved, in the people he loved. He brimmed over the edges of his own life, and escaped.

After Frederick leaves, I notice that Michael is sitting in the garden too. I walk over to him, and realize why he was silent. He's been crying. He didn't want us to see.

I say hello, but walk inside to let him have his privacy. I look at the Letter Library for a long time, thinking about the catalog, and how it doesn't feel like it's enough. Because a record on a computer doesn't show the way people have underlined. You can't tell from a database the deep mark that Michael left under Pip's words, telling Estella that she's part of his existence. *You have been in every line I have ever read since I first came here.*

That speech is underlined all the way through, and the notes in the margins are scribbled frantically. There's no way that I can record the reasons why people have underlined it or how they felt when they saw someone else had loved it before them.

I can't record the things I felt when I held the book. I can't record the worn pages or the coffee cup rings or the folded-down pages used to mark Auden's poetry. The feeling in the books is what Michael wants to keep, and a catalog won't do that for him.

I go upstairs to Henry. 'Wake up.' I say it close to his ear so my lips kiss his skin. 'Wake up. I know what we have to do.'

Henry

I wake and the world has not ended and Rachel is whispering transmigration into my ear. At least, I think that's what she's whispering. I'm distracted by her mouth, and the memory of what happened last night, and the hope that it might happen again, very soon.

I sit up and she says the word again. 'Transmigrate. The Letter Library has to transmigrate. We have to break it up and leave it in other bookstores.'

'It's a nice idea,' I tell her, but other shops won't take the books. 'It's Howling Books' thing. The books are written all over, so it's not like they can sell them. And if they kept them, all the books would do is take up valuable shelf space where they could put stock that they could sell.'

'So we won't tell anyone,' Rachel says, and I listen as she describes the operation. We disperse the Letter Library secretly, in all the bookshops around the city, and farther.

Pride and Prejudice and Zombies

by Jane Austen and Seth Grahame-Smith

Letter left between pp. 44 and 45

February 14, 2016

Dear Cal,

This isn't a good-bye letter; let's get that straight. I'll be writing more letters to you over the years. You've become the person I tell everything to, and that won't change.

I got your last letter – and the answer is yes. Yes, let's meet. Let's start at Frank's café for breakfast, and then we can go to the Palace, where I see they're having a Doctor Who marathon. Then we'll head across town to the museum, I think.

I'm not disappointed. I thought it was you – at least I was fairly sure, but then the letters kept coming after you'd moved, so for a while I wondered whether it was Tim. I didn't want it to be Tim. I wanted it to be you.

Do you remember that day at school when we sat out in the sun, watching everyone play? It was our first and only actual, not on paper, conversation.

I was crying because Mum wasn't at home anymore.

You: Hello.

Me: What do you want?

You: To make you feel better.

Me: Impossible.

You gave me the Sea-Monkeys.

You: They're fast-growing sea creatures. You put them in water and they grow really quickly. They get to be adults in about a week. They're not actual monkeys. They're a kind of brine shrimp. They start off as these cysts. If the conditions aren't good in the lake, the females release dormant cysts; the embryos just wait in those for as long as it takes for things to get better. And then, when things are good again, the life cycle keeps going. They're like time travelers, holding on till conditions improve.

Me: You're so weird.

You: I know.

I really loved those Sea-Monkeys, but I didn't say it then and I should have.

Love, George

Great Expectations

by Charles Dickens

Letter left between pp. 78 and 79

Dear Stranger,

If you have found this letter, then you have found this book. It's an incredibly important book - all books are incredibly important - but this book, this particular copy of this book, started a shop. Howling Books. Don't bother looking for it. By the time you read this letter, it will be gone.

This book was the first book on the shelf, the first book I gave my wife, and although we're no longer together, it is proof of how we loved each other once. Proof that we walked into a florist shop one day and dreamed into it another life.

So why haven't I kept it? A girl called Rachel convinced me I shouldn't. One morning, she found me crying in the reading garden. Weeping at the thought of my bookstore, my life, being knocked to the ground. It had been in our family for more than twenty years.

The bookstore is the building, but it's not only the building. It is the books inside. People are not only their bodies. And if there is no hope of saving the things we love in their original form, we must save them however we can.

Every single book from our Letter Library, all of them marked with lives, has transmigrated to another store. One by one, we snuck them into shops and placed them on the shelves.

Sometimes, the end begins.

Michael

Rachel

We spent the remainder of February working on the transmigration.

It's something you just have to get, Henry said. But I'm more scientific. I told myself that we were moving the books to preserve the memories in them, the thoughts on the pages. We secretly placed the books in other stores around the city, and at night, when I can't sleep, I like the thought that Michael's copy of *Great Expectations* now belongs to someone else. They are reading Michael's thoughts – his passion for Sophia, in the passion Pip had for Estella. His passion is there in his underlining, in his notes. In the inscription on the title page.

I have kept the Letter Library's copy of *Looking for Alaska*. It is to remind me that other people grieve and I'm not alone. I'm going to give it to Mum today, when we scatter Cal's ashes.

. . .

Henry drives us all to the beach for the ceremony – Lola, George and Martin are in the back. Sophia and Michael and Rose are following.

On the way to Sea Ridge, I'm thinking about the dream I had again last night. Cal and I saw the fish, those silver moons, unidentified. It changes, what I think those fish mean. I'll be puzzling over them all my life. But last night I woke and thought that maybe they're the questions, silver, strange and impossible to grasp.

I'm waiting for the water to appear – first in small triangles and then in deep scoops. Henry's looking a little worried, because I'm going back to the water that took Cal. It will be fine and it won't be. It will be terrible and good.

The past is with me; the future is unmapped and changeable. Ours for the imagining, spreading out before us. Sunlight-filled, deep blue, and the darkness.

Acknowledgments

Words in Deep Blue has been a team effort. Any mistakes are mine, but any good things about it are due to the help of a lot of very generous and very smart people. Thank you, Catherine Drayton, for being a brilliant agent and for having so much faith in me. Thank you to everyone at Inkwell Management, especially Lyndsey Blessing. Thank you to the wonderful Allison Wortche for all your time and effort, insight, intelligence and incredible attention to detail. Thank you, Karen Greenberg, Alison Kolani, Terry Deal, for all your help on the manuscript. Thank you to the designers of my beautiful cover, Alison Impey and Angela Carlino. Thank you to Stephanie Moss for the gorgeous interior design. And thank you to Barbara Marcus, Jenny Brown, Melanie Nolan, Kim Lauber, Jules Kelly, Cayla Rasi and Allison Judd for your support and your faith in the manuscript. Thank you, also, to my Australian editing team. Claire Craig, I could not have written the book without you. Ali Lavau, you are a brilliant editor, thank you, thank you. To my friends and family, who have stuck with me while this was being written – I really appreciate it. And of course, thank you to Michael Kitson.

BKMRK

Find your place

Want to be the first to hear
about the best new teen and YA reads?

Want exclusive content, offers
and competitions?

Want to chat about books with people
who love them as much as you do?

Look no further . . .

 @TeamBkmrk

 @TeamBkmrk

 /TeamBkmrk

 TeamBkmrk

See you there!

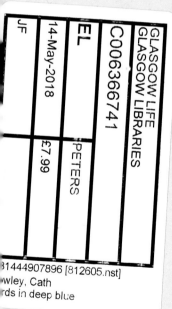

GLASGOW LIFE
GLASGOW LIBRARIES

C006366741

EL

14-May-2018

JF

PETERS

£7.99

81444907896 [812605.nst]
wley, Cath
rds in deep blue